INNER CITY

STORIES FROM THE THICK OF IT

INNER CITY

STORIES FROM THE THICK OF IT

Edited by
TONY BRADMAN

A & C Black • London

First published 2010 by
A & C Black Publishers Ltd
36 Soho Square, London, W1D 3QY

www.acblack.com

ISBN 978-1-4081-1376-9

A CIP catalogue for this book is available from the British Library.

Printed and bound Great Britain by MPG Books Limited.

Contents

Introduction
by Tony Bradman

I grew up in London, one of the oldest cities of them all, and have lived in its suburbs all my life. In fact, when I was born it was probably the biggest city in the world, although it soon lost that title to the super-cities of the late 20th and early 21st century, vast urban regions like Mexico City, Tokyo and Shanghai. So I know what city life feels like – streets filled with cars, the horizon obscured by rows of houses or office blocks, the sound of neighbours close by, huge crowds swarming into shopping centres or sporting stadiums, police sirens in the night.

That particular sound is often used on the soundtrack of TV shows or movies, to let us know they're about the tough side of city life. There's an easy link in many people's mind between cities and crime. The big city might be full of opportunities and entertainment, but there's a feeling that it's also full of bad people doing bad things, particularly in the centre, the inner city. That's where the slums are, the places where the poor people – often from a wide variety of backgrounds – live in terrible conditions, without any hope of a better future.

But that's not the way I remember it, and it's not what I've seen when I've visited schools all over the country. Sure, living in the inner city can be hard, but it can be interesting and lively and a lot of fun, too, and the people who live on unloved estates or in old tower blocks, in run-down houses and flats, are just as human as those who are lucky to live in more comfortable circumstances. One of the interesting things about this country is that the rich and poor often live quite close together, maybe even on streets that back on to each other.

So in this collection you'll read stories that explore the experience of living in the cities of this country and abroad. In T.M. Alexander's terrific story *Truant*, you'll meet Jackson from Bermondsey, a boy who needs a reason to spend his days at school, and finds one. In Julia Green's poignant story *What We Love* there's Suna, who has to come to terms with leaving the city for a new life in the country. Then there's Juca in Sean Taylor's marvellous story *Cutting the Air*, a boy in Brazil's Sao Paulo, who finds that just getting from one place to another can be a problem. But Robbie in Ian Beck's brilliantly original *It's All Right I Have a List That Helps to Make Everything Clear and It's Real Easy to Follow* deals with a similar problem in his own way.

In Alan Gibbons's hard-hitting story *Street without Windows,* crime does feature, and the neglect of the inner city, too, but its hero discovers that people can make a difference to their futures if they pull together. And in Joanna Nadin's *A Thousand Acres of Sky*, Luca loves the life he has in the country, but then has to move to the city, and discovers that it's not as bad as he thought it would be.

I hope that by the time you finish reading this book, you'll know much more about what it's like to live in the inner city. And maybe you'll find your story here, too...

A Thousand Acres of Sky
by Joanna Nadin

The Back of Beyond

If Mum was still alive, I know what she'd say. She'd say London is no place to bring up kids. She'd say it's dirty and dangerous. That the city chews people up and spits them out. If it doesn't swallow them whole.

Like the cancer swallowed her. The doctors tried to cut it out, but it kept growing until it ate her up.

So now she's dead. And I guess that's the point. Because if she was alive we wouldn't be going to live with Nan. We'd stay in Cornwall for ever. Where it's safe and clean. Where all you can hear is the wind. And all you can see is a thousand acres of sky.

The City

We're leaving tomorrow. Nan's taking us on the train with our suitcases and then Mr Mallin is going to bring all our other things in the van when he has to do a cheese delivery. I said I didn't want my trampoline smelling of cheese but Nan said there's no point in bringing it anyway as she doesn't have a garden just a concrete balcony, and if I try to trampoline on that I'll likely break a window or my neck.

Manny's dead excited. He says in London all the trains go underground and have actual real terrorists on them. Plus Nan's television has 47 channels and some of them just show cartoons ALL DAY. We don't have one channel, or even a television, because Mum said it would limit our imaginations. Although Rory Polmear has a television and he says he has seen a vampire so I don't think *his* imagination is very limited. But that's not the point.

I told Manny about the chewing up and spitting out but he just said cities can't chew because they don't have actual real teeth. Nan says he's pretty smart for a six year old, but he still believes in Father Christmas so how smart can he be?

Anyway, it's OK for him. He's a kid. It's different when you're ten. Everything's different. Like school. I don't think the school in London has just thirteen people in it all in one class, even Sasha Pritchard who is four and falls over all the time. There'll be thousands, maybe millions of children and I won't know a single one. And I won't be living next door to Finn any more, so how will he still be my best friend? What if he starts being best friends with Danny Roberts who has a quad bike. And what if he forgets to look after Lulu? What if she runs away and tries to find me in London? I asked Nan if I could bring her but she said the fourth floor of Essex House was no place for a chicken and she'd start pining for the yard and get ill and stop laying. I said what if I started pining and got ill? But Nan said I didn't lay eggs so it wasn't the same and besides, she couldn't leave me behind as legally I need a responsible adult in charge of me. I said what about Dad? But she said Lordy, Luca, if there's one thing your dad is not, it's a responsible adult. I said how did she know, as he hasn't been home since Manny was born. Nan just rolled her eyes then and told me to pack my suitcase.

So I did. I packed my clothes and my Ordnance Survey map of the village and Mum's emergency money jar which has nearly eleven pounds in it, and a picture of Mum holding Lulu and laughing because Lulu was flapping her wings and trying to fly. And I looked really hard at the photo, and in my head I heard her. Mum. She said, 'Don't cry, Luca. I'm coming with you.'

Essex House

The train didn't go underground. It stopped at Paddington and then we got a bus and Manny started crying because he wanted to see the terrorists so Nan said she'd take him on the tube tomorrow and they could go round and round all day if he liked until he'd spotted one. He cheered up a bit then. Plus the bus had two layers on it and we went on the top one and you could see Hyde Park and the MI5 building. Which was OK, I suppose.

But I wasn't really looking. I was looking at the millions of people and thinking I didn't know any of them. And none of them looked like anyone from our village. In our village everyone has the same kind of skin and hair and even clothes, except mostly the men don't wear skirts. And Rory Polmear is ginger and his skin is so white it's almost blue. But in London there are hundreds of colours of skins and kinds of clothes.

Even in Nan's block of flats in Peckham the people are all different. Nan is in number 4b and in 4a is a man from the Ukraine, which is where Russia used to be I think, and on the other side in 4c is a family from Nigeria but they've only been there a month and Nan says before that there was a lady from Macedonia, which I didn't even know was real. Manny said maybe the man from the Ukraine was a spy. Nan said maybe. Although mostly he works in Blockbuster video so she's not sure how much spying he could get done there unless it's to see who rents James Bond films.

Nan's flat has five rooms. A living room, which has a dining table in it too, a kitchen, a bathroom and two bedrooms: one for Nan and one for me and Manny. I said me and Manny had our own rooms at home but Nan says unless I want to sleep with her, which she does not recommend because she snores like a walrus, or in the bathroom, then it's Manny or nothing. I don't want to sleep with Nan. Or in the bathroom. It is purple and smells of perfume and Manny says it is like a witch's lair. I don't believe in witches but I'm still not sleeping in there. There isn't even an upstairs. Even the bus had an upstairs. At home we had an upstairs and an attic, which is where my bedroom was. The window was on a hinge in the slanting roof and you could swing it open and be standing right in the middle of the sky and you could see for ever.

I went on Nan's balcony to see if I could see for ever. But there was just another block of flats that looked exactly the same as ours, and a car park with a goal post painted on one wall and some teenagers leaning on it, and a dog that was doing a poo and no one picked it up. I looked up at the sky and it was tiny. And there weren't even any stars. Because of all the lights in the city, Nan said. They shine too bright and drown out the planets. Then in my head I heard Mum. And she said, 'But what's the point of living somewhere where you can't even see the stars?' And I knew she wouldn't stay.

London
We went on the underground today and Nan

showed us the stations that were bomb shelters when she was a little girl, and the ghost stations that aren't actually haunted but are ones that no one uses any more but there are still platforms and tiles spelling out their names and you can see them if you squint into the darkness in the right places. Manny says he saw five terrorists and when he grows up he is going to be a tube driver so he can go round in the tunnels all day.

But all the time we were going round and round my brain kept thinking about the city chewing people up and spitting them out and I know London doesn't have teeth but it has tube stations that swallow people down and spit them out again in a different place. And then I wondered if everyone *did* get out or if you could get stuck on the tube for ever and then I felt like it was swallowing me and I said to Nan I wanted to get off and she said OK, Luca, I think two hours and thirty seven minutes is enough for anyone, even Manny, and anyway I need a wee so what say we go to London Zoo? And so we got off at the next stop and I held my breath all the way up the escalator until the tube spat us out into the sunshine.

The zoo was huge. Not like the one we went to at school in Mrs Holloway's minibus, which just had two otters and some flamingos only you couldn't see the flamingos because they had flu. This one had lions and tigers and deadly snakes and a beetle as big as your hand. And there was a bit where you could walk with the monkeys only Manny got shouted at because you are only supposed to walk with the monkeys not pick them up in case they catch a disease and die, so I don't see where the fun is in that. Nan asked if we wanted to see Pet's Corner because they have goats and even chickens and you are allowed to touch them. But I said I didn't want to see any more animals that are locked up because animals are meant to be free and wild, like Lulu who was allowed to go where she liked, even down to the village and someone would always bring her home at night. And Nan said that's OK in the village but no one wants goats or monkeys or tigers wandering down Oxford Street, and the animals would just get run over so the zoo is the best place for them. And I thought that's not what Mum would say. And I listened in my head again to hear her. But she was quiet. And I thought maybe she had gone already.

But she hadn't. Because when we got back to the flat Nan put on the telly and it was Power Rangers which I know about because Rory has a Power Rangers suit that he wears all the time even to school some days and Nan said we could eat our tea on the sofa. And then I heard her. She said, 'It'll rot your brain, Luca.' And even though a bit of me wanted to see Power Rangers, I didn't want Mum to go home. So I said I needed some peace and went to our bedroom and lay on my bed.

But I didn't get much peace because Nan came in with a plate of Marmite sandwiches and a bag of Hula Hoops and sat down on the end of my bed. She said you'll grow to love it, in time. And I knew she meant the city. I said no I won't. You can't see the stars, and the animals are all locked up and you can't touch them because they're not supposed to be here. They're in the wrong place. They should be in the country or the desert or the jungle where there aren't any buses to run them over or people to get scared. That's where home is. And I thought Nan would be cross but she wasn't, she just smiled and said there's more to

London than the zoo, Luca, you'll see. It's a city full of secrets. Like the ghost stations. I'll show you tomorrow. But you need to eat your tea.

And I did. But not all of the crisps. Because Mum said crisps should be a treat.

The Magical Mystery Tour
When I came out of my bedroom for breakfast there was a black man and girl sitting at the dining table. Nan said this is my friend Otis and his niece Asha from 5c upstairs. She's ten too so she'll be in your class at school, Luca. I looked at Asha and she had stuff in her hair to make it shiny and earrings and nail varnish on and she looked a lot more then ten. She looked like Danny's sister who is 13 and at secondary school and has kissed three boys. Manny said are you a terrorist? And Otis laughed so you could see his gold teeth and he said no I'm a bus conductor, and today I'm taking you on a magical mystery tour, boy. And Manny said are we really, are we going on the bus? And Asha laughed and Otis said no, we were walking as it was only round the corner, which didn't sound too magical or mysterious to me.

And it wasn't. Not at first anyway. It was

Peckham Rye, which is a big park, but the grass is all burnt and there is a lot of dog poo and litter. So Nan said stop looking down, Luca, you'll always be miserable if you look down. Look up at the sky. So I did. And then I saw one. A flash of bright green across the cloud. The kind of green that is lime jelly or sherbet. The kind you never see on normal birds. Manny said is it a parrot? So I said don't be stupid, parrots live in zoos or in cages. But Otis said Manny, you not far off, boy. It's a parakeet. Look, there's a whole flock. And we looked really hard. Like we were squinting in the dark at the ghost stations, and then they appeared: tiny flecks of sherbet green in the oak tree. Hundreds of them. Then Otis made a whooping noise with his hands round his mouth and they all shot up into the air and swooped in an arc towards the ground, then up again before they landed back where they started.

Why are they here? I said. This isn't their home. And Otis said they not born here, but this is home now. They found a way to live. Jus' like me.

Then Otis took us to see the Ninja Turtles in the pond. Which was just an ordinary pond with ducks and stuff, except that when you looked closely the rocks moved and turned into giant turtles. Nan said there were dozens in there, because people bought baby ones thinking they were cute like the cartoon, and then they got too big for their tanks so they just dumped them in the pond. And even though it wasn't the Red Sea or wherever they came from, they had carried on growing and eating fish and were happy. Except for the shopping trolley and the drink cans which Nan said were a disgrace.

On the way back Manny asked Asha if anyone had a gun or drugs at school. She said she didn't think so but that Shanice in Year 6 once ate a Pritt Stick and was sick in assembly. Then Asha asked what it was like in our village. And Manny said it was boring because there wasn't any telly or Hula Hoops. But I said it was magical. And mysterious. And that the wind was so strong sometimes you could stand diagonally without falling over, and you could see a million stars, even shooting ones sometimes. And Asha said I could be your friend, if you like. And I said it's OK I've still got Finn. But then I realised maybe I didn't. Maybe he was on Danny's quad bike right now. And I felt really sick. Like when you've been on a roundabout too long. And I listened hard in my head for Mum to say something nice. But she didn't say anything at all. All I heard was Asha going whatever.

Home

When we got back I said I really needed to phone Finn to check that Lulu was OK. And I thought Nan would say no but she said that's fine, Luca, what's his number? And I said he hasn't got one, you have to call Mrs Housden at the post office and she'll go and fetch him. Nan said what a palaver. But she did it anyway.

Mrs Housden stayed on the phone for ages telling me about how one of Mr Mallin's cows got loose and came into the post office and ate a box of cereal and a pair of rubber gloves before they could get her out and in the end I said please can you get Finn now and she said she would just be a jiffy, which was actually more like seven minutes, because I checked on Nan's gold clock. But Finn was there, he wasn't out with Danny. He said what's it like? Is it brilliant? Have you seen the Queen? Are there actually terrorists on the tube? And I said no, but not anything about hating it because Nan was in the room and even though she can't hear everything I bet she'd be able to hear that and anyway I wanted to know about Lulu so I asked him if he'd given her grapes every day and clean water and had he made sure she had fresh bedding because otherwise she would get cross and lay her eggs in the bushes and then it takes hours to find them. But Finn said it's just a chicken, Luca. And I heard someone else speaking and Finn said I've got to go. Danny's here. We're going to play football. And then the phone made a long beeping sound and I knew he'd hung up. And even though it was football not the quad bike the sick feeling came right back. And I listened again for Mum. But she wasn't there. And I knew why. I knew she'd gone home. And I knew I had to go back too. To Finn, to Lulu, and to her.

The plan
I'm going to do it tomorrow. I'm going to get the 36 bus from the end of the road to Paddington and then get a train back to Bodmin. Then I can just call Mrs Housden and tell her to get Finn and then his dad can get me in the Land Rover. Or I could even walk. I know the way because it's

on my Ordnance Survey map. I asked Manny if he would come with me but he says he'd rather stay here because of the 47 channels and the underground and the Hula Hoops. It's a good thing really, as I don't think there's enough money in Mum's emergency jar for two train tickets. Plus he moans if he has to walk very far.

I've packed my *Harry Potter*s and T-shirts and jeans back in the suitcase. I'm leaving the photo of Lulu and Mum though. That way Nan won't realise I've gone for a bit longer if I leave something precious. And anyway, I won't need the photo because this time tomorrow I'll be with them again.

I thought she'd come back for a minute. Mum, I mean. I went out onto the balcony and looked at the acre of sky with no stars and I listened hard into the wind. And at first it just brought sirens and car engines and voices I didn't recognise, shouting and laughing. Then I heard something else. A voice calling up Luca, Luca. And I saw an arm waving and white teeth and the glint of gold earrings in the dark of the car park. But when I looked again I saw it wasn't her. It was just Asha. So I waved and went back inside.

Going home

It totally went to plan. Or at least it did for the first hour and twenty-six minutes.

I waited until Nan was watching *Homes Under the Hammer*, which is her all-time favourite TV programme, and Manny was drawing a picture of a Power Ranger with Nan's lipstick, then I listened really hard at the front door to make sure no one was outside, especially the man from 4a in case he really is a spy. I couldn't hear anything so I knew it was time, only when I opened the door Asha was sat on the stairs opposite. She said where are you going, Luca? Are you going on holiday? I said kind of. She said can I come? I said no, it's not that kind of holiday. She said please, you can say you're playing at mine and I'll say I'm at yours. It's foolproof I've seen it on *Hannah Montana*. And I had to admit it was a Brilliant Idea even though I don't know who Hannah Montana is. Maybe she is a spy too. So I left the suitcase in the hall and went to tell Nan I was going to Asha's. She said that's nice, Luca, you've got one new friend already. Soon you won't miss Finn at all. I said yes, even though it was a lie. Because sometimes you have to lie to stop feeling people sad. Then

I gave her a kiss and she smelled of perfume like the bathroom. She said blimey, Luca, you're only going upstairs. I laughed then but it was a scared kind of laugh and I looked at Manny. But he was eating the lipstick and didn't even look up.

When I got back into the hall Asha was there with a purple shiny handbag and a packet of biscuits. For the plane, she said. Because it cost five pounds for a sandwich on the plane when I went to Mallorca and I don't have five pounds I only have two pounds fifty-three. I said I had more than eleven pounds but that we weren't going on the plane we were going on the number 36 bus. Asha said oh, like she was really disappointed. So I said it's actually quite good because you can see Hyde Park and the MI5 building and you can sit on the top deck. Then I remembered that Asha gets the bus all the time. So I didn't say much after that.

The bus didn't come for ten minutes and I had the sick feeling the whole time in case Nan had realised about the Brilliant Idea and come to find us. But she didn't and we got on the bus and went straight up to the top and as we drove down Peckham High Street, past Bottles off-licence, and the Job Centre and the Persian shop, I felt the sickness dissolving. And I knew it was going to be all right.

Except it wasn't. Because we had only got to the Marbella Hotel when a man's voice said Asha, what you doin' goin' to town, chuh? And I looked up and there was Otis in his conductor uniform staring at my suitcase and I knew he knew, and then the sick feeling came right back again only much worse and I thought I was actually going to be sick. And Otis looked at me and he said this our stop, boy.

When we got outside Otis didn't say anything he just started walking. So we followed him, up a tall hill of big white houses until we got to the top and he went up to the front door of one of the houses and pushed it open. I whispered is he a burglar? But Asha made a sucky sound with her teeth and said no, he lives here, innit.

Otis's flat was at the top of a tall rickety staircase. It was warm and dark and smelled of cinnamon and lemons. He opened a door at the end of the kitchen and I thought it must be a door to nowhere and I started to feel scared again. And I remembered what Mum had said about talking to strangers and about bad men in the city. But Otis looked at me and said it OK, Luca. Come. And I did. I walked out but it didn't go nowhere. It went somewhere. Everywhere.

Otis's roof was a garden. But not a normal one with grass and a swing. It had mirrors and palms and a lemon tree. And it was better than any garden I'd ever seen. Even ours in the village. Because this one was on top of the world. I could see for miles and miles, across the whole of the city. I could see skyscrapers and gold-topped mosques and the London Eye like a giant Ferris wheel, and Wembley's arches.

You think I born here, boy? Otis said. I born in Trinidad. Where it hot all day, and the air smell sweet and a man can breathe. But I find a way to live. To breathe. And now this my home. Look up, boy. You see.

And I looked. And I saw it, all around me. It was there all the time: a thousand acres of sky.

Home
Otis didn't tell Nan. He just took us back to Essex House and said he'd be watching us like a tiger watch a monkey.

But he didn't need to. I knew I wouldn't hear Mum again. At least not all the time. But maybe she'll come back once in a while to check. Because when I stood there, up on the roof, I felt the same as I did when she would smile at me, her hair swirling in the wind, her arms out, her head tilted back, saying a thousand acres, Luca, look, a thousand acres of sky and it's all ours.

And Otis lets me and Asha go up to look at the sky whenever we want. At night is the best. Because Otis says you don't need stars when you've got all the city lights. And he's right. It's beautiful. On bonfire night we all went up, Nan and Manny and Asha and her sister Keisha. And we watched the whole of London under a cloud of falling fire in pink and gold and green. I think Mum would have liked to have seen that.

Finn rang as well from Mrs Housden's. He said Lulu got lost for two weeks but Mr Mallin found her in his milking barn and she had four chicks underneath her and they are called Donatello, Raphaelo, Leonardo and Michelangelo, after the Ninja Turtles, even though three of them are girls.

And best of all, we're going to get two of them, me and Asha. Mr Mallin is going to bring them up when he next does the cheese. Otis is going to make a special house for them in his roof garden. He says they'll love it up there with all the plants and the fresh air.

He's right. Because, even though they weren't born in the city, they'll see the good stuff. And find a way to live.

It's All Right I Have a List That Helps to Make Everything Clear and It's Real Easy to Follow
by Ian Beck

1. Leave School

At the 3:11 pm tick by the laptop icon, another fat raindrop slid down the window. Robbie watched with fascinated concentration as the last drops raced one another. First they fell against the glass and rolled down the clear part at the top of the window, and then the drops turned into lines on the lower frosted area. If he looked upwards and away from the laptop screen he could see clear-blue sky behind the moving clouds among the buildings. Little patches of blue sky. The empty blue air filled the spaces left by the clouds themselves. He knew the name for that kind of cloud. They were called 'cumulus'.

'Next please, Robbie.'

He turned back and clicked through to another picture. He used the space bar to go forwards. He could have used the forward arrow instead, but he preferred to use the space bar.

The clock on the laptop showed the time, 3:12 pm. Soon they would stop for the day. He would get to number 2 on the list.

Danno had whispered 'mad kid' at break, had whispered it right at him. Danno had come up close, grinning right in his face, and Robbie had felt the muscles in his neck tighten and he *screamed* right back in Danno's face. He had clenched his hands into fists and he had bared his teeth like some baboon, and with his eyes closed tight he had hit out at Danno, hit him over and over.

Danno and Robbie were sent to the principal's office. Mr Groszinski rolled up a piece of paper into a ball while he spoke.

'This is the very last time,' he said, pointing at Danno. 'You will be excluded, finito, kaput, if it happens again.' Then he threw the ball of yellow paper into the novelty mini basketball hoop, which had been suckered onto the side of the grey filing cabinet. He raised his arms, in celebration.

Robbie was sent to the quiet place. He was left to sit there on his own for a few minutes, to think about what he had done.

'Next please.'

Robbie pressed the space bar very carefully, and then sat up straighter in his chair. He could hear the raindrops, their slow fading tap on the window. He knew that it would brighten up soon by the amount of blue, by the exact ratio of blue colour to white clouds, only a shower.

He shut down the laptop. He took out the memory stick and put the cap onto it, and then handed it over.

'Well done and thank you, Robbie, that was all the better for a little politeness and quiet, do you see that?'

Robbie nodded, looking down at his trainers. His bag and his list were in the corridor in his locker. He waited for Danno, the grey-hooded wolf-boy, to leave. He watched him go out, banging the classroom door, and then he waited again. He counted to one hundred and then he went out to the corridor. He went to the locker. He took out his bag while a flow of noisy students pushed past him. He unzipped the side pocket and then he took out the list and the pencil. He put the bag over his shoulder, felt its weight and held the folded list ready with the pencil. He walked down the corridor to the double swing doors at the entrance.

He waited in the corner.

Every time the doors opened, he looked out to see if the rain had finally stopped. He had only to look at the asphalt directly outside. It was wet and glossy but the surfaces of the pooled puddles were quite still now and reflected nothing but blue. He looked outside at least twice as other people left. And every time he checked the surfaces of the puddles, they remained glossy and still, like oil.

Finally, he stepped outside. He could smell gas, cars, cooked onions, hot-dog meat, hot bricks and fresh wet air. He unfolded the list and put a tick with the pencil against number 1, *Leave School*. And then he folded up the list again.

2. Walk to Station

Parents and students milled around outside the gate. Some wore bright plastic raincoats and some still had their umbrellas up.

'It's stopped raining,' Robbie said loudly to no one in particular as he came out of the narrow gate and pushed through them, squeaking against the wet slicks.

They stood aside quickly to let him pass.

RVs were banked up, double parked, revving engines. Loud music, a dance track came from a black-windowed Jeep. The deep bass notes thumped out as Robbie passed and he hated his feet for trying to fall into the trap of walking to the skanky rhythm. This was not his kind of music. Steam rose visibly around him off the hot pavement as the shower evaporated.

Robbie looked up and tracked the sky as he walked. It was all-over blue now. It followed him, looked back down at him in luminous patches through the bricks and high concrete. The distant rippling clouds were just bright-white cumulus now. The heavier grey clouds had moved further away eastbound. It was a short walk to the elevated L-train station.

He noticed wolfie Danno hanging out, under the bridge. He could see him in the shadowy part.

The bridge was wide, and was dark underneath even on a bright afternoon. Danno, with his hood flipped up, now had a Yankees cap pulled down low over his eyes. He was waiting, prowling with three of his wolf friends.

Robbie stopped and took his bag from his shoulder. He unzipped the side pocket and put the list and pencil back in. Then he set off back up the street and waited, catching his thoughts behind the thumping black-windowed car. He heard a train rumble and clatter over the bridge. It was not his train though, it was a westbound. He needed the eastbound. But he couldn't go under the bridge and up the steps to the eastbound side because of Danno and his wolves.

Robbie had screamed at Danno and then he had hit him, and now Danno was waiting to get him back. That was the rule, a rule which he half understood. He knew now what he had to do. He heard Danno shout something, heard him roar, a threat, a beast noise, followed by the wolf-boys laughing. They had all seen him now.

Robbie tried hard to pay no attention. He kept his eyes on the ground where the sunlight burned bright on his white trainers. The beat-box thump thump of the Jeep's stereo was annoying him. He was agitated now, feeling a little hyper. He could feel himself tightening, as if the air was being sucked out of him and he shrunk tight into himself. He was torn, worried about getting too close to Danno and getting far enough away from the thump thump bass noise that hurt his ears, hurt his mind. He would have to choose between them.

An elaborate old-fashioned iron-sided staircase ran up both sides of the bridge. Robbie was sure that the stairs were dangerously loose, they wobbled like baby teeth. They were so old that they would surely collapse and spill him back down into the street one day. He could picture the stairs tumbling and the bridge and the tracks and east and westbound trains tumbling down with them, too, all crashing across the road into the traffic. He could see it so clearly. If he could sneak across to the nearest staircase, he could at least get to a platform without passing Danno and his wolves.

There were plenty of people on the street to mask him. He stepped out from behind the Jeep onto the pavement. The sun was brighter now, slanting between the tall buildings, casting shadows and dazzles on the details of cars and trucks. Danno and the others were still there under the bridge, like a stain. Robbie tucked into a shop doorway, hoisted his bag from his shoulder, unzipped the front pocket and pulled out his i-Pod and headphones. He plugged himself in. Bach, a cool fountain of notes, a piano, it always calmed him right away. The bright street floated quietly around him, suddenly stilled to the new soundtrack. He put his bag back over his shoulder and stepped out into the sunlit stream. He watched his feet as he went towards the steps. He kept close behind a blimp-shaped man walking with a hot dog in a greasy paper napkin trailing sweet onion smells behind him. A dog on a long chain lead suddenly leaped up from the passing crowd barking and slavering at the hot-dog meat. The dude with the dog yanked the chain and the dog was caught up short, legs dangling like Spike in an old *Tom and Jerry* cartoon. The blimp laughed at the dog as it was dragged past, and

Robbie barked in imitation, causing the blimp to turn.

'Oh, real funny, kid,' the blimp said through a food-crowded mouth.

Robbie reached into the bag and put a pencil tick next to number 2, *Walk to Station*.

3. Get on Train

Robbie dance-dashed up the steps on the wrong side of the bridge. The enemy remained unaware. No wolves howled out to him. He flew up the steps light as down with the clean notes rising in his ears. He stood on the westbound side. The sunlight caught on the tracks, the eastbound platform was busier. A westbound came in, and sighed to a stop at the platform. Robbie waited as the doors hissed open and then saw Danno through the double layers of window, and Danno saw him. Robbie stepped into the carriage and hung onto a strap, bending to look over at the eastbound platform. They were there lined up; Danno bright in the sun while his three wolves stood further back in the shadows.

The westbound lurched off and Robbie turned to the station list on the map – three stops and then a triple interchange at Roosevelt where he could turn and go back on an eastbound.

He hefted his school bag, unzipped the pocket, took out the list and ticked number 3, *Get on Train*.

4. Ride on Train

Robbie stayed on his feet, ignoring the empty seats all around him. He allowed himself to go with the train movement as he dangled from the strap. He arched himself up and stood on tiptoes. He lurched around as the train cornered, and then he swung back again, and it seemed in his head, in his ears, that it was all in time to the steady pulse of the music. He reached down and pulled the list from the bag and quickly pencil ticked, with a dancer's flourish, number 4, *Ride on Train*.

At Roosevelt he got off and switched over to the eastbound platform. The train pulled in, busier in this direction. He took a seat next to an abandoned newspaper and switched his i-Pod to shuffle. He smiled at the woman in the opposite seat, and she scowled at him as the train went back through the same stations. He could look down into offices and apartments.

He caught snatched flashes of afternoon lives: a man peering at a screen, a group smoking outside on a fire escape. The train rattled into Hamilton and there they were, still on the platform, Danno and his wolf pack.

Robbie laughed too loudly and his laugh was sudden, like the barking dog.

'It's stopped raining,' he said, to no one in particular.

The woman opposite nodded but her mouth stayed straight across her face, and then after a moment she got up and moved across the aisle to another seat. The train stopped and passengers got on. One of them picked up the newspaper and others settled on the few empty seats one at a time, keeping themselves to themselves. Robbie smiled at them anyway. The train moved off again.

He noticed the connecting door between the carriages had suddenly come open and no one went to shut it properly. It kept slamming bang and opening again and every time it banged, he shouted out 'bang', and laughed.

Danno and the three other wolf-boys came through into the carriage.

Robbie took a bow and arrow out from the other zipped side pocket of his bag. He stood up and screamed out loud at them all and his face reddened as the wind rushed through the carriage from the open connecting door. The wind swirled some sheets of newspaper into the air and he fired a steel-tipped arrow at Danno. It landed right in Danno's chest, in the dead centre of his cruel heart and his wolf blood flowed out over the floor.

Of course, that didn't really happen. Though he saw it happen in his head. He *wanted* it to happen.

What really happened was he just sat there and looked out of the window. He was trying not to notice them. That was hard to do as the wolves stood together in a pack near the slamming connecting door, all swaying off balance and dancing against the music in his head as the train moved around the bends. They were all grinning, teeth shining, daring him to look back at them. Danno still had his hood up and his face was in shadow.

'It's stopped raining,' Robbie said, keeping his forehead touching the glass of the window but watching them in the reflection.

'Stopped raining, you say?' Danno said. 'Stopped raining has it, crazy kid?'

'What were you thinking?' said one of his hooded wolves.

He turned towards them and adjusted the bag on his shoulder.

'I wasn't thinking,' he shouted out, widening his eyes.

'What were you thinking when you thought you could get away with hitting me?' Danno said, stepping forward and leaning over him, holding onto the hanging strap as he rolled around in a direct parody of how Robbie had stood westbound minutes before, going with the flow and movement of the train.

'You crossed the line,' Danno said.

'I wasn't thinking about that,' Robbie said, staring out of the window at a Bagel Factory outlet and not looking at Danno at all.

'You don't think, do you?'

'I do think. I think the rain has stopped,' he said.

Danno sat down in the empty seat opposite. He put his trainers up on the seat next to Robbie.

'You shouldn't be allowed out,' Danno said, and kicked at Robbie with his elaborately laced shoe.

Robbie took no notice.

'Are you listening?' Danno said, and kicked out again.

Robbie nodded. 'Bach,' he said loudly.

'Like a dog,' Danno said and high-fived one of the wolves.

The train stopped. Two of Danno's hooded wolves sloped off and more passengers and umbrellas got on. A guy in a wet-patched Dr Pepper T-shirt asked Danno to 'move his **** feet'. Danno seemed to shrink as the guy brushed hard at the seat with a rolled-up newspaper, saying to Danno, 'I'll come and dump my stinking feet all over yo mamma's couch, shall I?'

Diminished, Danno stood up. He said nothing and went and hung beside his remaining wolf, glaring over at Robbie. Out of the window, the white cumulus clouds looked higher and further away.

Robbie rested his head on the glass. He tilted his eyes upwards and watched the clouds as they dodged between the spires of the city, sunlight and deep shadows and bright windows reflecting the light in neat squares. The train rattled to the next station. He knew that Danno would get off, but he stayed in his seat looking up at the sky. There was a sudden bang on the glass by his head as Danno punched the window as he walked past.

'Tomorrow,' the wolf mouthed at him through the glass.

Robbie stayed looking upwards.

Two stops later, he got off. He took the list from the zipped pocket and put a second tick by number 4, *Ride on Train*. Then he folded the list, put it back in the zipped pocket, adjusted the bag and set off down into the street.

5. Walk Home

Robbie walked up the main avenue where the sidewalk was still wet. He crossed over and stood outside the front of his building. He took the bag from his shoulder and took out the list and put a tick by number 5, *Walk Home*.

He went through the lobby, nodded to García at the desk, who smiled and pointed to his own ears and then nodded. Robbie barked like a dog, and Garcia smiled and put up his thumb. It was a little thing they had.

47

Robbie opened the door with the list still in his hand. In his mind, his mum came out from her study, she waved at him then held up her finger for him to wait, and so he stood where he was and watched her so clearly as she walked to the kitchen and picked up something. She came back down the hallway and held out both hands to him. In one hand she held a milk carton ('Missing' it said in red letters, 'Sven Nikvist of St Paul Minn'. There was a photograph of a blond boy) and in the other she held a packet of cookies. The image dissolved as the track in his head ended. He took the headphones out of his ears, unplugged the i-Pod and went through to the quiet musty kitchen. A fly buzzed around the bin. He turned on the kettle and went and looked up out of the window above the well of the building. The sky was still blue. He looked down at the paper in his hand. He ticked the last entry on his mum's list, number 6, *Milk and Cookies*.

Truant
by T.M. Alexander

Tiffany

If you asked me how I decide whether or not to go to school, the answer would be complicated. First there's the weather – who wants to be in school when it's sunny? But I can't stay at home if Kash (Mum's boyfriend) is at ours. I tried once but he got up and dragged me there. Arriving at break with a bodyguard was *not* cool. What sort of mood I'm in – that makes a difference. And whether I've got any money. Money's important – no money means school, for definite. Unless I bump into someone like Joel on the way and *he's* got money and we bunk off together.

So it's complicated.

But that Wednesday it was pouring and I was broke and Kash was there, so it was school.

And that was the day I met Tiffany.

(Don't worry – it's not a love story. Tiffany's a rabbit.)

(Only joking – Tiffany's not a rabbit, she's a person, but it's still not a love story.)

Our fill-in teacher, Miss Bassett, is much better than Rogers. He was a total wimp. Whatever went wrong, he never tried to sort it out. He never asked anyone what had happened or why, so most of the time he got the wrong kid. Usually me. And if not me, Sam. Or sometimes both of us. The minute any trouble kicked off, it would be, 'Outside, now!'

So we'd go outside.

Right outside.

Outside the class.

Outside the playground.

Outside the gates.

That's when I started missing school.

What was the point of turning up if you only got sent away?

Pat in the school office rang to find out what was wrong, and Mum told her I got lots of headaches. Then the Education Welfare Officer got involved. The first time she came, Mum was still in bed (she works nights) and I was down The Blue. (Everyone calls it that. It's where all the shops are, and the market.) The second time we were watching telly.

Mum answered the door.

The truancy woman said, 'Well, Mrs Murray, you know why I'm here.'

And Mum said, 'He's ill.'

And she said, 'Can I see him?'

'In there,' Mum said.

She came in and asked me if I was ill, and I nodded.

'He looks fine to me,' she said to Mum. But Mum didn't hear because she was watching Jeremy Kyle.

'I said, he looks fine to me,' the officer said again, really loudly.

And Mum said, 'He's being bullied.'

Where did that come from? I thought.

Anyway, because of that the officer spoke to the school and they asked me all about it, so I told them about Rogers, because I couldn't think of anything else to say.

He's gone now – Rogers. Someone said he'd got a brain tumour but Mum says he's off with stress.

She thinks all teachers are rubbish and go off sick the whole time because they can't cope. I don't know how she knows because she never comes to parents' evenings. She never goes anywhere much, except over to Becca's. And on Saturday nights her and Kash go up the Blue Anchor. I stay home and watch telly till late and get a pepperoni pizza with extra chilli – Kash gives me the money and I keep the change.

It's only Miss Bassett's third week but she knows our names. And she's funny, which is odd for a teacher.

'Hey, kids. What sort of day are we gonna have today?'

See what I mean? She's supposed to take the register and start the lesson, but Miss Bassett asks everyone a question like 'Sam, what did you have for breakfast?' or 'Aria, what's a Komodo Dragon?' It's better than asking us if we're here!

I don't mind school so much now, but it's boring to go every day. I can read and do maths and I don't need to know about fat kings or riverbanks. The only river I know is the River Thames and that doesn't have otters, it has rats, and the sides aren't mud, they're concrete.

That Wednesday, Miss Bassett got to my name, Jackson Murray (I come after Maeve Lisle and before Kyrial Najir), and my question was 'So, Jackson, where were you yesterday?'

'Ill, Miss.'

'And what particular illness was that? Lie-in-bed-itus? Telly-itus?'

'Headache,' I said. She knew I was lying. And she knew I knew she knew. I didn't care though.

'Well, it's nice to see you today,' she said, and smiled. See, she's a big improvement. No threats. Nothing, just...

'And if you get a headache tomorrow, come in anyway and I'll teach you how to massage headaches away. OK?'

'OK,' I said, but I don't think she was serious...

At lunch time, I played football with Aria. *He* never misses school.

'What did you do yesterday, Jackson?'

'Went over the skate park with Joel.'

Joel is *meant* to be in our class, but he never is. He's either at home, over the park or in the empty flat where his brothers hang out. It's the middle one on the top floor. From the walkway, you can see people go in and out, but it's not a good idea to stare. Not unless you want a row. I've never actually been up there, but I know all about it. Mum says I should keep away. All the mums say that. We don't need telling. Everyone knows about the squat.

'You should have come,' I said, but I was only joking. I often am.

'My dad would kill me,' said Aria. 'He says the only way to get a Subaru Impreza Turbo is a good education. He says he didn't come to London so his kids could end up taking the bus.'

Aria's dad is strict.

'Whatever,' I said.

Aria likes cars. And he wants to be a vet. You don't get a lot of vets around our way. But there are lots of dogs so I suppose we could do with one.

After lunch we did the 'reading together' book. It's about a boy in the war who goes to live with an old man to avoid the bombs and then he goes back to his mum but she's a headcase and eventually the kind old man finds the boy again and it all works out. I liked it – got through it in two afternoons.

'Your turn to read, Sam. Do you know where we are?' (He never does.)

'We're at school, Sam,' I said.

'Thank you for that, Jackson,' said Miss Bassett. 'Top of page 63, Sam. Off you go.'

Some of the kids in our class don't know much English. (Mum says half of Bermondsey doesn't.) Aria's mum comes in twice a week to help them read. On the other days, Miss Bassett tries to make them understand the story by using sign language. Not proper signs for deaf people – made-up ones. It's mad. But it's fun, too. We've started acting things out to help.

I think the way we all joined in, rather than looking out the window (me) or playing with phones under the desk (not me – mine got nicked), might be what gave Miss Bassett the idea to ask Tiffany to come in.

'Hey, class. Listen up. This is Tiffany and she's going to talk to you about drama. So no messing about ... as if you would.' Miss Bassett looked over the top of her glasses, but she didn't look scary. She can't.

And neither did Tiffany. She looked like ... a celebrity!

'Hi, everyone, I'm Tiff.'

She talked about herself, but I don't remember

what she said because I was too busy watching her arms flying around. She was better than telly – all bright colours and … electricity.

'So, over to you now. I want you to tell me your name, the name you'd call yourself if you could choose, and something you're good at.'

Most kids said ordinary things, or stupid things like, 'I'm Jack and I'd like to be called Razorman'.

Except…

'I'm Aria, and I'm happy to be called Aria because it's me. I'm good at cooking mutter paneer and I hate artichokes.'

I've never tasted an artichoke or heard of mutter paneer. Sometimes Aria seems like he's from Jupiter.

And…

'I'm Maeve and I'd like to be called something long, like Esmerelda or Francesca. I'm good at gym and I go to a club and I want to be in the Olympics.'

Maeve is good at everything.

Then it was my turn…

'I'm Jackson. But I wouldn't mind being called…' I thought of something posh. 'Ralph. And I'm good at…'

There was a blank where there should have been an idea.

'...jokes.'

'Excellent,' said Tiffany. 'Tell us one then.'

I wished I'd said something else, like wrestling. She wouldn't have made me do *that* in front of the class.

I stood up and took a deep breath. 'What does Geronimo say when he jumps out of a plane?' It was a bit lame... I looked round, expecting someone to shout out the answer.

'We're on the edge of our seats,' said Tiffany.

The joke was getting less funny by the second ... oh well!

'Meeeeeeeeeeee!' I shouted and spread my wings – I mean arms.

Tiffany let out this big noise. It wasn't a laugh. It was a *roar*. Everyone else was completely quiet. They didn't get it. That made it funnier in a way, and I started laughing. We laughed for ages, just me and Tiffany.

Finally, she stopped and explained the punchline to the rest of the class.

'When people jump out of things they shout "Geronimo", so when Geronimo does it, he shouts…' She stopped to laugh a bit more. 'He shouts ME!'

No one made a sound.

'I think you need to shout it, Miss, and spread your wings,' I said.

'It's Tiff, not Miss. And thank you, Ralph. I think you're right.'

It was weird, like we were on the same wavelength.

Alice went last. She said she'd like to be called Tiffany. We all pretended to be sick.

After that Tiffany put us in pairs and one of us had to move and the other one was the mirror. We were messing about, me and Sam, so she came round and made me do it with her, and she was incredible. It was like she knew what I was going to do because she did everything at *exactly* the same time as me. I tried to trick her by moving really fast, but she was there – every time. If I believed in them, I'd have said she was a witch.

The bell went. I thought it was the fire alarm, but it was already home time.

'Starting tomorrow, I'm going to be running a drama club in the hall. You're all welcome. Four o'clock till five thirty.'

The girls immediately went into a huddle, like they do.

I pushed past.

'Bye then, Ralph,' said Tiffany. 'See you tomorrow.'

I nodded, but I don't know why. I've never joined a club and I wasn't joining drama.

Maeve

I got a bowl of Cheerios and ate them in front of the telly. I *was* planning on going to school, but I ended up just sitting there. And then Kash came lolloping out and when he saw me he looked at his watch, clobbered me round the head and shouted, 'You're late, Jacko.'

'Leave me alone, that hurts!' I yelled.

It didn't, but I thought Mum might hear.

'Get a move on, Jacko,' he said. And pushed me out of the door.

'Why should I?'

'Because I say so. Because you're meant to be at school.'

I didn't like the look on his face, so I scarpered. If I'd seen Joel I'd have gone off with him, but I didn't, so I went in late.

'Funny time to turn up,' said Miss Bassett. 'Another headache?'

I didn't answer. I was really angry. Kash is *not* my dad, and it's *not* his home, it's *mine*.

After school I waited in the playground to see what Sam was doing, or Aria. (Not that I go over to his much ... I don't think his mum likes me.) I didn't want to go home in case Kash was still there. He doesn't have a normal job so there's no telling when he's going to be around.

Tiffany cycled through the gates.

'Hi there, Ralph. You coming?'

I couldn't see anyone else to muck about with so...

Why not? I thought.

The minute I got into the hall, I decided it wasn't for me. There were fourteen kids – ten girls and four boys. Maeve and Alice were there but no one else from my class. And I wasn't in the mood to 'be a tree, swaying in the wind'.

'Two things. One – call me Tiff. Two – we're going to play a game to stop us all staring at each other wondering why we've come.'

I was about to walk out – I didn't want to play a silly game – when she said, 'So, Jackson aka

62

Ralph. You're Killer Tic.'

I could have gone, ignored her and put one step in front of the other but ... she'd laughed at my Geronimo joke and she was smiling so...

'What do I do?'

It was like tag but more complicated. I was 'it' and had to catch the others. Simple. If I touched them, they were it, but if I got near and they shouted the name of someone else before I got them, that person became the Tic instead. To start with, we were all over the place and no one knew who to run away from, but then we got quick and it was wicked. No one caught me, not once.

We played loads of games, and didn't do any drama, but it was good.

On the way home, some of the kids from the other school were hanging about outside the shop (Joel calls it 'the cage' because of the metal grills). I crossed over the road.

'Hi,' said a voice from somewhere behind me.

It was Maeve. She lives in one of the new houses past the estate. It's because her mum's a nurse. Mum says it's rubbish the way the ones with the good jobs – the nurses and the teachers – get help, and people like her who sort parcels all night when everyone else is asleep don't get nothing.

I waited until I was well past the shop before I crossed back over. Maeve came, too. We walked the rest of the way by the river (you can see Tower Bridge, and a bit further along you can even see the London Eye), and came out round the back of the estate.

Joel was up on the walkway between Eden House (where he lives) and Lee (where I live).

He shouted down, 'Where you off?'

'Home,' I said.

'Come up here.'

'No,' I shouted. 'I'm hungry.'

'Suit yourself.'

'Why do you bother with him?' said Maeve.

'He's a mate,' I said shrugging my shoulders.

'He's trouble,' she said. 'You know who his brothers are, don't you?'

'Course,' I said. Everyone knows them. They're called The Stick and Edge – street names.

'So you should stay away.'

'Joel's all right,' I said.

'Says who? Sam's sister says he's a runner for the squat.'

I didn't want to know. Running about fetching and carrying for the guys in the squat meant something bad. Something the Fedz would be interested in.

'We only go to the skate park,' I said. 'No one's ever been shifted for doing a kickflip'. Joel's a diamond skater. He can flip 360s either way.

She made a face.

'What do you think of Tiff?' I said. I didn't want to think about Joel, or Kash, or Mum.

'I think she's amazing and I love the way she talks, it's like singing. You going next week?'

'Might do,' I said.

Maeve put her floppy fringe behind her ear, 'You only pretend to be cool, Jackson Murray. I know you want to go really – teacher's pet.'

I tried to kick her, but she jumped out of the way.

'Bye,' I said. We were at the entrance to my block.

'Bye.'

Mum and Kash had a massive row when they got back on Saturday night and he hadn't been round since, so I didn't go to school on Monday or Tuesday. I was watching breakfast telly on

Wednesday when the bell rang. I thought it was the truancy lady again, but it wasn't, it was Maeve.

'Come on, dope. Get dressed.'

I was wearing a dressing gown that used to be Mum's. I couldn't stand there talking to Maeve in a *dressing gown* so I did what she said and as I was dressed I thought I might as well go with her.

'Why haven't you been at school?' said Maeve.

'Because.'

'That's not an answer.'

'I know.'

'Doesn't your mum make you?'

'No. She's asleep, and even if she's awake, she doesn't care. Says it's a waste of time.'

'She's wrong though, isn't she?'

The way Maeve said it made me stop and think. I didn't know if Mum was wrong or not. I know you're *meant* to go to school, but I wasn't sure why. If you can read and write and add up, why do you need to know about evaporation or French? My mum can't even say *bonjour*. School just keeps us out of the way and gives us free dinners.

Maeve must have got bored with waiting for me to answer. She jumped up onto the wall that runs past the park. I did, too. She ran along it even though it's only as wide as my foot. I tried, but I fell off. Maeve's like a mountain goat. I've never seen a mountain. I bet they're higher than the flats.

Miss Bassett had a word with me at break. I felt a bit sorry for her – she seemed to think there was something up. While she was droning on, I was thinking that if she wanted someone to help, there were plenty of kids I could suggest. I mean, Josh still wets himself!

'...children often think that no one cares, but that's simply not true.' She stopped and looked at me so I assumed the chat was over.

'It's all right, Miss,' I said. 'No one's died.'

My nan used to say that – before she died. (Only joking. She moved to Manchester, near my aunty Helen.)

At drama we played Target. I was made for it. Fast, eyes in the back of my head, determined not to be had. Maeve was pretty good, too. We were sweating by the time Tiff called time. I was ready for more games but we did this balancing thing where you had to lean against each other and not fall over. I was with Maeve and Alice.

It was getting a bit too tree swaying for me ...
until she showed us how to stand strong. It's to
do with getting three points on the floor – the
ball of your foot, the heel and the outside. It
sounds obvious, but before she showed us she
could push everyone over using only one finger.
Afterwards, when she tried, we were all rock solid.

Once we'd got the hang of that, two of us held
the other one in a lift, without them weighing
anything! Me and Maeve lifted Alice and then
they did me. And I was safe as houses.

I walked back with Maeve. And this time I ran
along the wall but didn't fall off. It was like my
body knew where it was.

'Do you want to come to mine?' she said.

I've never been inside one of the new houses.

'No, thanks,' I said. 'I'm going home.'

'What about Saturday?'

'Maybe,' I said. I don't know why I said that.
I wasn't going. They're not our sort of people.

As I went in the door, I heard Kash. He must
have made it up with Mum. I went straight
back out.

'Jackson!'

I looked over the railing – Joel was down

below, so off I went. We got some chips and ate them at his. And then his mobile rang.

'Yep. Already done, Bro,' he said.

He flipped his phone shut.

'Coming?' he said.

I looked at all the stuff in his front room, and on him. A telly as big as the wall, loads of DVDs, flash phone, trainers, money in his pocket.

'Sure,' I said.

Joel

I knew where he was going – right up to the top. The no-go zone. I followed him. In the last stairwell the bulb had gone so I couldn't see anything, which somehow made me notice the stink more – it comes from the bin bags people just dump ... and worse stuff. We came out onto the landing and I took a gulp of fresh air.

'You all right?' said Joel.

I nodded.

He knocked on the door of the empty flat – three raps.

His brother, Edge, opened the door.

'Junior,' he said, and rubbed Joel's head as though he was a dog. (He is a bit like a dog. One with a temper ... a Rottweiler.)

'Hi,' said Joel.

'Who's your mate?'

He nodded in my direction.

'Jackson. He's all right.'

I tried to look as though I wasn't bothered. Wasn't bothered about being let in or not being let in. Not bothered about who he was or what they were doing or what Joel was going to do or whether I was going to do it with him.

'Coming in?' he said.

Joel walked in, so I followed. I didn't think about what Mum had said or about what was going to happen next. The door went straight into the front room. There were four others in there. Joel went over but I didn't get what was going on because my feet were stuck to the floor. (Not really stuck, with glue. Not working. *I* wasn't worried ... but maybe my legs were.)

Joel took some money and shouted, 'Back in a bit.'

He shoved me towards the door. It slammed behind us and we were off.

'What was that all about?' I said.

'They want some stuff from the cage.'

Joel ran down the stairs but I hung behind. What sort of stuff?

'If you don't want to come, Jackson, go home.'

I thought about it, but I didn't go home. Because Kash was there. And because I'm not chicken.

We walked back the way I'd come – down behind the flats and along by the river. There was no one about. Joel went into the shop and bought biscuits and crisps – birthday party food! (Not that I ever have one.)

'Is that what you do? Get the shopping? Where's your trolley, Joel?'

I laughed.

'Laugh if you like, loser. But at least I know what I'm at.'

'So what?' I said. I don't know what I meant. Or what he meant.

Joel rapped three times again. His brother took the bag and the change and gave Joel two fivers.

We went back down the stairs and stopped under the walkway. He waved the notes in front of my face.

'I'm making money, Jackson. What are you doing? Wasting time at school.'

He put the money in his jeans pocket, and then he changed his mind.

'Here you go.'

He gave one of the notes to me. I took it.

'Thanks,' I said.

It was getting dark. I ran over to our block, took the stairs two at a time and charged into the flat. I didn't care if Kash was there.

I had five quid in my pocket.

Kash

On Saturday I had a lie-in. When I got up there was no noise in the flat and no milk, so I went to get some.

'Jackson!'

Joel was there with his skateboard, so I went back and got mine.

His phone rang a couple of times but he didn't rush off anywhere. I was half hoping he would, so I could share his earnings. Shopping was easy money. And then it rang again. This time he didn't speak, just listened.

'Got to go,' he said.

He flicked up his board, caught it and put it under his arm.

I stood there like a lemon, but not as yellow.
'Coming?'

I picked up my board and we ran off.

Up the steps. Whiff of rotting rubbish. Back out in the light. Rap rap rap. Just like before.

The door opened.

I turned and looked out over the estate, not because it's interesting, but because I was trying to look cool. And that's when I saw them. One minute it was a normal day, the next there were heads popping up and out and bodies moving, but no sound. If you lived somewhere like me, you'd know what was going down. And suddenly I didn't want to be anywhere near the squat.

I ran.

I ran down all the flights of stairs (almost missing a couple of times), across the grassy bit between the blocks, up the back stairwell and in the door, smack into Kash.

'What's the panic, Jacko?'

I shut the door behind me, panting.

'What's up?' he said.

I didn't want to tell him. But I had to tell someone. Because I'd left Joel. And I didn't think the police would believe he was getting biscuits.

'Is Mum here?'

'No. She's round at Becca's. What is it, Jack?'

I thought about running over there, but I wasn't as scared of Kash as I was of what was going on over in Eden.

There was some shouting. Kash opened the door, looked out over the railing and shut it again. I don't know what he saw, but I could guess. It wasn't the first time there'd been a raid.

'You'd better tell me where you've been.' This time he meant to get an answer.

'I was at the squat – not *in* it. Outside.'

'With that Joel?'

I nodded.

'Jackson, you're playing with fire. You know that, don't you?'

'We didn't do anything.'

'Listen to me.' He jabbed me with his finger. 'If you go on missing school and messing about with Joel, you'll end up in trouble. They'll have you marked, Jacko, and one day you'll be shoved into the back of a van and end up in the nick.'

He put his head in his hands, as though he had a headache, and stayed like that. I didn't know what to do. You can't talk to someone who's staring at their knees.

There was the sound of boots on the stairwell, lots of them. Kash sat up and listened, like a deer does when it thinks it can hear a lion or a hyena, or whatever it is that eats them.

I didn't breathe. I don't think he did, either.

Were they coming to get me?

Jackson

Things have been a bit different since that day. Not really different, like I'm now a prince and live in a mansion with flat-screen tellies in every room and a swimming pool. But better than they were. Well, better for me. Not for Joel. Turns out it wasn't *only* shopping he was doing. He's in care now.

Kash was mad for a bit, which was quite lairy, but then we struck a deal. I have to go to school every day and in return I get to choose something to do at the weekend, like go up Surrey Quays and see a film, or go bowling, and we do it. (It was the truancy lady's idea.) Suits me, as I'd already decided not to bunk off any more anyway – partly because Miss Bassett asked me not to, but also because me and Maeve have been working on something. And for that I need to be at school.

It's all to do with Tiff. She dragged the Head along to drama club when we were doing our routine and next thing it was agreed we'd be part of this community performance at the Unicorn Theatre where Tiff works – and it's tomorrow!

We've been practising like mad. The thing we're doing is like a mixture of break dancing and gymnastics, and the music really pumps. Everyone in the drama group's doing something different, but it all goes together. We had a rehearsal yesterday in front of our class and Aria said, 'It rocks'.

'So what's the plan this weekend, Jacko?' Kash asked me.

'You've got to come and watch us do our thing at the theatre,' I said.

'Not bowling?'

I shook my head.

'How about the pool in Deptford?'

'No, I've already said, haven't I? We're going to the theatre. You've got to be at the Unicorn at two thirty.'

'To watch you and that Maeve?'

'And the others,' I said.

I waited to see what he was going to say. There was no point asking Mum, because she never comes to anything. *All* Maeve's family are coming – even aunties.

'Well, Jacko, if that's the plan, I'll be there. Sitting at the front watching you make an ass of yourself with that crazy girl.'

He didn't mean it. Maeve and Kash get on all right. She came home with me the other day. I didn't ask her, she just tagged along. Kash got us pizzas.

On Saturday, Maeve came to get me and we walked there together. We had to be at the theatre for half-past one to rehearse on the stage. It wasn't even one so we were stupidly early.

'I've got that weird wobbly feeling in my tummy,' she said.

'No need,' I said. 'There'll probably only be two people watching.'

'There'll be a least seven,' said Maeve. 'And they'll all be staring at me, but I've told them not to wave.'

I laughed at the thought of Maeve's family sitting in a row waving. That would put all of us off.

'There'll be eight actually.'

'Why? Is Kash coming?'

I nodded.

'Wicked,' she said.

I thought about that. No one had ever come and watched me do anything before. In fact, I'd never done anything anyone *could* come and watch before.

'Yeah, wicked.'

Street without Windows
by Alan Gibbons

I walk to school down a street without windows. They're all boarded up. It started about a year ago. Workmen would arrive and put up metal screens or plywood boards. It wasn't long before the glass panes stopped shining in the sunlight. Soon the window cleaners stopped coming round with their ladders and buckets. The old ladies no longer twitched at the curtains to see what was going on in the street. I walk faster now than I used to. There was a time I would gaze at the windows and try to imagine what the house was like. My mate Chris and I would make up stories about the people inside.

'Maybe a footballer lives in that one,' I said.

'Don't be daft,' Chris shot back. 'Footballers live behind high walls. Their houses are so far back you can't even see them. Footballers wouldn't live round here. Where would they park their Bentleys?'

'What about a player in the reserves?' I suggested.

'Don't be stupid,' Chris answered. He pointed to a house with peeling paint on the window frames. 'See that one? I reckon a bearded lady lives there. She's got a bearded dog and a bearded cat and she's got a wicked laugh like this ... whooo ... hoo ... hooo.'

Chris thinks he's some kind of comedian. His laugh is more like Santa Claus than a bearded lady.

'You're turning into a bearded lady yourself, you great numpty,' I snorted, then we had a play fight all the way to the school gates.

We do that sort of a thing on a good day. Other times it feels like we're walking through a ghost town and we stop talking altogether.

The older kids have started spray-canning their tags on the boards. It makes the street look kind of scary. There's one tag we see everywhere: Gonz. He goes to the high school just down the road from our school. Gonz is a real psycho.

Just lately, Chris and I have started walking really fast down the street without windows. Its proper name is Newgate Street but everybody calls it The Tin on account of all the metal screens. Once you get to the streets around The Tin, you know you're in the badlands.

When you turn right out of The Tin, you're on the Parade. That's where the shops are. There's a mini-market, a chippy, and a shop called Everything for a Pound. There used to be a post office, but it shut down. There was a butcher's shop, too, but that's gone. There are more boards where they used to be.

There's one building with lots of shiny windows though. That's the library. They've got a kids' reading group and I go on a Thursday after school. Chris says I'm a boffin. I don't care. I like it. There's about ten of us and we all read the same book then spend half an hour arguing about it. There's always juice and biscuits. Gill runs it. She's one of the librarians. Mum says librarians are supposed to have glasses on chains, but Gill's got black lipstick, purple hair and a stud through her nose. There's this girl Lauren who goes. Dead bossy she is. She only likes books about ponies and stuff. When we read about spies or monsters, she turns her nose up. One time she was getting on my nerves so much I told her they eat ponies in France. I wanted to wind her up. I thought she would cry, but she waited until we were outside and punched me on the nose. Whatever happened to sugar and spice?

I was on my way home one Thursday after the reading group, when I saw Gonz and two of his mates sitting on the garden wall. They'd kicked half of it down and there was rubble lying in the overgrown garden. If Dad had been there, he would have got on his mobile to tell the police what they'd done. He's always going on about how the decent people need to claim back the estate from the scallies.

'You live on Braddock Way, don't you?' Gonz asked as I came closer.

I hesitated for a moment, then I answered, 'Yes, that's right.'

I don't live anywhere near there, but I wasn't about to tell Gonz. I didn't want him knowing where he can find me, did I?

'What number?'

'66.' I said it without thinking. It just popped

into my head. You know, like 666, the sign of the Beast. Gonz is a Beast.

'I might come round your house sometime,' Gonz said, winking at his mates.

They all started laughing.

'What would you want to do that for?' I asked, my voice shaking a bit.

I hoped they wouldn't notice, but they did, of course.

'Are you scared of me?' Gonz asked.

'No,' I said.

He leaned forward. His breath smelled of cigarette smoke and too many days not brushing his teeth. 'Well, you should be,' he said.

Then he made a grab for me and I pegged it. I could hear them roaring their heads off behind me. I didn't stop running till I got home.

Mum asked me why I was in such a hurry. I told her I wanted to watch something on TV. She didn't believe me, but she didn't give me the Third Degree. She's good like that. She doesn't go on at me much.

I'd almost forgotten about my run-in with Gonz and his mates when I ran into them again. I was with Chris this time.

'Oh, great,' I groaned as we turned the corner from the Parade.

'What's up?' Chris asked.

Then he saw Gonz.

'Well, if it isn't our friend from Braddock Way,' Gonz said, winking at his mates. 'Only you don't live on Braddock Way, do you?'

'I do,' I said, 'don't I, Chris?'

Chris was staring at me, wondering what I was up to. He decided to play along. 'Yes,' he said. 'That's where he lives, Braddock Way, by the Fire Station.'

'What number?'

I tried to mouth the number.

'You come over here,' Gonz ordered.

I shuffled forward a couple of steps. Now Chris couldn't see my face.

'What number?' Gonz growled. He glared at me. 'No turning round, you.'

That's when Chris said it. 'Number two, just like you.'

I just stared at Gonz for a moment. His face went purple.

'What did you say?' he yelled.

'Number two, you lump of poo!' Chris yelled. Then he ran off, leaving me standing there with my mouth open.

Not for long. I quickly spun on my heel and fled down the street. I'm not as fast as Chris, and Gonz and his mates were getting closer. I could hear their trainers pounding on the pavement. I raced round the next corner in pursuit of Chris. I'd just run past an alley when a wheelie bin trundled out into Gonz's path. He fell and sprawled on the ground.

'Don't just stand there gawping,' Chris shouted. 'Move!'

We lost Gonz two streets from my house.

'You nutter!' I shouted.

'Who are you calling a nutter?' Chris demanded. 'I stopped you getting done over.'

'Yes,' I shot back, 'straight after you nearly got me done over in the first place. What were you doing calling Gonz names?'

'He would have hit us anyway,' Chris said.

'You don't know that,' I protested.

'Yes, I do,' Chris said.

Deep down inside, I knew he was right. There was something bothering me, too. Why did Gonz want to know where I lived?

The next Thursday I had something else to worry about. I got to the reading group and Lauren was very upset. Her eyes were red and she was blowing her nose into a Kleenex.

'What's up with you?' I asked. 'Did your pony die?'

I wished I hadn't said it, but you can't put words back in your mouth.

'I don't have a pony,' she said angrily. 'It's the library. They're going to close it down.'

'What do you mean?'

'Gill just told me,' Lauren said. 'The council wants to shut it.'

'They can't do that,' I said.

Gill arrived with the juice and biscuits. 'They can, you know,' she said.

'Does that mean there isn't going to be a reading group any more?' I asked.

'No, we'll keep it going,' Gill said.

Something about the look on her face told me there was a but.

'It's going to be at Central Library,' she said.

'Do you mean the one by the Town Hall?' I cried. 'My parents won't let me go there alone.'

'Maybe they can take you,' Gill said.

I shook my head. 'They both work. They don't get home in time. It's not fair.'

'You're right,' Gill said. 'It isn't.'

'Somebody should do something about it,' I said.

'The lad's right,' said a voice behind me.

I turned round. There was this old guy sitting at one of the computers.

'We should do a petition,' he said. 'Yes, we could take it down the Town Hall.'

'Could we do that?' Lauren said, brightening up.

'I don't know,' Gill said. 'Maybe.'

We did it. Mum wasn't keen on me going to the Town Hall at first. Then she met Jack, that's the old guy. He was with his wife Sue. They got a group going to save the library. They made signs and got loads of signatures. Once Mum was satisfied that they were OK, she said I could join their group. The evening we went to the Town Hall there were about two hundred people. Fifty of them were kids like me. Even Chris turned up.

'What are you doing here?' I asked. 'I thought you said people who read books are boffins.'

'They are,' Chris said, 'but our Jess goes to the homework club there.'

Jessica's his big sister. She's another boffin. She wants to go to university. Chris's parents are saving up for a computer. Until then, Jess has the homework club at the library.

The day after the protest at the Town Hall I ran into Gonz again.

'Well, if it isn't 66,' he said, stepping out from an alley as I made my way down The Tin.

'That wheelie bin did my knee, you little rat.'

'I wasn't the one who pushed it,' I said.

'No, your mate did,' Gonz said. 'Where is he?'

'Football training,' I said. My heart was pounding.

'Maybe I'll wait for him,' Gonz said, gazing down The Tin towards the school.

'There's no point,' I said quickly. 'His dad picks him up. He doesn't like him walking home in the dark.'

'Is that right?' Gonz asked.

He thought I was lying and he was right.

'You don't want to get on the wrong side of me, you know,' he said.

I didn't say anything.

'You see, I like getting my own way.'

Still no answer.

'I know where you live.' He told me the address. I swallowed hard. 'You wouldn't like a brick going through the window, would you?'

I shook my head.

'I mean, it could hit your mum or that little sister of yours,' he said. 'How old is she, five, six?'

'She's six.'

Gonz smirked. 'You never know, I might strike lucky and hit your grass of a dad.'

He knew all about the family. And why did he call Dad a grass?

'I don't want any trouble,' I said.

'There won't be,' Gonz told me, 'if you play along.'

'What do you mean?' I asked.

'I want you to keep something for me,' he said.

I didn't like the sound of that.

'What is it?'

'You don't need to know,' Gonz said. 'It's just something I want to put in a safe place. I can't keep it at home, see.'

This was really freaking me out.

'I won't do it,' I said.

Gonz's eyes narrowed. 'So you want a brick through the window, do you?'

I shook my head.

'Or maybe you'd like a good kicking instead?'

I shook my head again. 'Why don't you leave me alone?'

'I don't want to,' Gonz said. 'The next time I see you, I'll have a little package with me. You're going to keep it at your house. Put it somewhere safe. Don't go blabbing to your parents, either. It wouldn't be good for your health.'

I had a sick feeling in my stomach. How had I got into this mess? Why did Gonz have to pick on me? I decided to start walking. Maybe he'd just been winding me up. I'd only gone a few steps when Gonz gave me his parting shot.

'I'll be looking out for you,' he said. 'See you soon.'

I found it hard to sleep that night. I just kept tossing and turning. Chris knew something was wrong the next morning. I tried to clam up, but eventually I told him what had happened.

'What do you think he's up to?' I wondered out loud.

'Beats me,' Chris said. 'One thing's for certain. It can't be legal.'

'What should I do?' I asked.

'The same as me,' Chris said. 'I'm going the long way home from now on.'

'We could do that,' I said, encouraged. 'It'll take ten minutes longer though.'

'What's that to you?' Chris asked. 'Your parents don't get home until six o'clock. They're not going to know any different, are they?'

He was right. Nan picked up our Katie and they went to her house. Mum collected Katie from there when she finished work.

For a few days we stayed out of Gonz's way. Then Gonz came looking for me. Yesterday, he caught up with me by the Fire Station.

'So this is where you've been hiding yourself,' he drawled, darting a hostile glance at Chris.

'Look, we don't want any trouble,' Chris said, backing away.

'This is your lucky day,' Gonz said. 'I want a word with my mate here. You can clear off.'

Chris looked at me uneasily.

'You go,' I said, trying to sound braver than I felt. 'I'll be all right.'

'Are you sure?' Chris asked, still not moving.

'Yes, I'm fine.'

'By the way,' Gonz said, pointing a finger at Chris, 'this doesn't mean I've forgotten the wheelie bin. I'll be having a word with you about that.'

Chris swallowed hard. As he wandered off down the road, my flesh was crawling.

'You've been avoiding me,' Gonz said.

'No, I haven't,' I protested. 'It's just that I –'

'Shut it!' Gonz snapped. 'I don't like people lying to me.'

He made a grab for my jacket and dragged me over to the side of the Fire Station. He slammed me into it so hard my teeth rattled.

'You listen to me,' he growled. 'You're going to be a good little boy and do exactly as I say. Remember that package I wanted you to keep for me, I've got it here.'

'What is it?' I asked.

'You know what they say,' Gonz said. 'Curiosity killed the cat. Take it!'

I tried to struggle free. 'I don't want it!'

'Cut that out,' Gonz snapped. 'Either take it, or I'll give you some of this.' He shoved his fist in my face.

'Let me go,' I protested.

'All you've got to do is this one little thing,'

he said, relaxing his grip, 'and then I'll be off your back.'

'You're really going to leave me alone?' I asked.

Gonz nodded. He held out the package. It was wrapped in grey duct tape. 'Take it,' he said.

I hesitated. He smirked and turned his back. I watched him leave and made my decision.

That was yesterday. I still shake when I think about it. Gonz is really bad news. I wouldn't put anything past him. I'm on my way to the Town Hall again. Mum says I can get the bus there by myself, but Dad's going to pick me up after the protest. It's the night the council is going to make the decision about our library. Jack says there are going to be hundreds of people inside this time, arguing their case. I should be looking forward to it. The trouble is, I can't get Gonz's stupid, ugly face out of my mind. I never really believed him when he said he was going to leave me alone. He's never going to let go.

The moment I get off the bus I see Jack and his wife. They come over and Jack shakes my hand. Me, an eleven year old kid. Jack's like that. He treats everybody the same.

'Good turn out, isn't it?' he says.

Jack was right about the numbers. There must be three or four hundred people carrying banners and placards and balloons. Some of them have got whistles and they're making a terrific noise. I should be enjoying it. But all I can think about is Gonz.

'Are you all right?' Jack asks.

'Yes,' I say. 'I'm fine.'

'You don't look it,' he grunts. 'Anyway, there's a favour I want to ask.'

'What is it?' I ask.

'The TV crew want to talk to one of the reading group,' Jack says. 'Lauren was going to do it but she's lost her nerve.'

'Are you telling me Lauren's scared of something?' I ask, amazed.

'Well, she doesn't want to talk to the telly,' Jack says. 'What do you say?'

I agree to do it. For a while we chant and sing and try to talk to the councillors as they go in. Then Jack comes over with a man and a woman. The woman is carrying one of those clipboard things. The man has a camera perched on his shoulder. I do the interview. To be honest, I really enjoy it. The words just come to me. I tell them I want the library to stay open because nearly everything else is closed down. I say I'm sick of walking down a street with no windows. They seem pleased with that. I'm just finishing talking when Dad arrives. He listens for a moment then smiles as the TV people walk away.

'That was really good,' he says putting his arm round my shoulders.

'Thanks,' I reply.

He pulls out the evening paper. 'Your mate Jack's in here saying why the library should stay open.'

I look at the article, then my eyes widen.

'What's wrong?' Dad asks.

I point to the photo of Gonz on the opposite page. 'I know him.'

'How?'

It all comes flooding out, all the stuff I've been keeping secret. And now it's Dad's turn to look shocked. 'This guy's in court for burglary and some other stuff. Why didn't you say anything?'

'He said he'd brick the house,' I explain.

'So he wanted you to keep something for him, did he?' Dad asks.

'I took it,' I say.

Dad rolls his eyes, but before he can say a word, I tell him the rest.

'But I didn't take it home.'

'Thank goodness for that,' Dad says. 'I've got history with this young thug. He wanted to plant something on me so he could get me in trouble with the police.'

'I don't understand,' I say.

'I once called the police about a trouble-maker on the estate,' Dad says.

The penny drops. 'Gonz?' I ask.

'Yes,' Dad says. 'I shopped him to the police. He was trying to use you to get back at me.' He glances at the photo. 'It didn't work though.' He pauses for a moment. 'What did you do with that package?'

'I threw it away.' Dad raises an eyebrow and I tell him where. 'The metal screen is loose on one of the derelict houses. I shoved it in there.'

Dad looks interested. 'Do you think it's still there?'

I shrug. 'Probably.'

Dad waves the newspaper article. 'Our friend Gonz is in a pile of trouble already. If his fingerprints are on that package, he could be in a whole load more.'

A big roar goes up from the crowd. It's time to go in and hear the council's decision.

'Let's see what they've got to say,' Dad says. 'Oh, and next time something's wrong, don't bottle it up. Tell me.'

I nod. 'Are you going to tell the police about that package?'

'Oh, yes,' Dad says. 'I'll call them the moment the meeting's over. Are you OK with that? You're not worried about him?'

'No,' I say. 'I'm not scared any more.'

And I'm telling the truth.

With any luck, I've got Gonz off my back. I did the right thing dumping that package. I look at the crowd. It's good knowing this many people care what happens to the neighbourhood. If we win tonight, it's a start. Maybe one day The Tin will be back to normal, not a street without windows.

Cutting the Air
by Sean Taylor

The cars and buses were hardly moving along my
street. An ambulance had its siren and lights going
but it was stuck, the same as everyone. I ducked
into the shade of the passage round the side of
the bakery and banged on Deni's door. After a bit,
his cousin, Robson, opened it. I stayed outside.
Deni's family's so big, by the time you've gone
round saying hello to everyone, you're late for
football. And if you're late, Senhor Jonas won't
let you train. He says showing up on time and
warming up properly are the first things you've
got to learn if you want to be a professional.

'What you doing here, Juca?' asked Deni.

'What d'you *think*?' I said, pointing at my team
shirt. 'Are you coming?'

'Football's not till four o'clock.'

'It's good to get there early,' I told him.

Deni grabbed the bag with his kit in and jumped down the steps.

'Why? So you can polish Senhor Jonas's boots and iron his underpants?'

'Go have a bath!' I told him.

'It's true!' laughed Deni. 'Now you're captain, you suck up to him every chance you get!'

That was Deni's usual hot air. He was jealous. Things were going well. The team was winning. Senhor Jonas had got us proper shirts. We were in the quarter finals of São Paulo under-12's. And if we won, it was me going to lift the cup.

Deni wasn't in the team any more. Once he'd turned 12, Senhor Jonas said he had to try to get into the under-13's.

'Senhor Jonas shouldn't have kicked me out of the team,' said Deni, with a sniff. 'I'm the step-over wizard. All the other coaches just say their players are still eleven, even when they're 12.'

'Senhor Jonas won't do that.'

'He's got a screw loose,' shrugged Deni. 'Have you got money for the bus?'

I nodded.

'What about you?'

Deni tutted. 'No one had any spare. But I know how to get the bus without paying.'

I grinned. It was easy when you'd done it once. And Deni and I had done it lots.

'If you do it, too, we can get hot dogs with your bus money,' he said.

I didn't even need to think. There was a hot-dog man up by the weirdo hairdressers. You could help yourself to all the extras you wanted.

Out in the street, the cars were moving again. The ambulance had got past. We dodged over to the hot-dog stand. My bus money was enough for a hot dog each. We went crazy with the extras ... mayonnaise, salt, ketchup, mustard, mashed potato, crisps. Then we ate in the shade, on the steps of the hairdressers. There were two women inside and it creased us up laughing every time we looked round. One had pink dreadlocks sticking out the top of her head. The other was bald except for a bit of blonde hair flapping down the side of her face.

I was hungry and I finished my hot dog quickly. Deni was having a bit of trouble with his. Every time he took a bite, globs of ketchup and mayonnaise dripped onto the steps. Then the woman with the pink hair came out.

'WHO'S GOING TO CLEAN THAT UP?' she said. 'GET OUT OF HERE!'

'D'you wanna bite?' asked Deni, holding up the hot dog.

'I don't know how you can eat that disgusting stuff,' she told him.

'I don't know how you can walk around with a pink bird's nest on your head!' I said back.

Deni burst out laughing. The woman swung a leg as if she was going to kick me. I jumped up, but she didn't do it. She shut the door. I wiped some ketchup off the step and used it to draw a picture of her on the window. Then she flew outside again and nearly *did* kick me.

'Sorry!' I said, swerving out the way. 'It was an accident!'

A bus was going past. It was ours.

'Come on!' I shouted.

'I'm eating!' complained Deni. But he got up and ran after me.

There wasn't anyone at the stop, so the bus carried on. We chased after it. I nearly knocked over some crack-head poking about in a pile of black sacks. Deni was behind me. I didn't think

104

we were going to catch the bus. But it had to stop at the lights. I cut between the cars and got on. And don't think I mean I got *in*. I jammed my fingers in the gap between the green panel and the back window, and pulled myself up. Then I got my trainers on the ridge of the white panel that runs between the brake lights. It was harder for Deni. He had to keep his football bag on his back *and* hold on to what was left of his hot dog at the same time! He managed though. We kept our heads down so that the driver couldn't see us. And the bus was off.

I smiled because the driver pulled away really fast. Then we were out of the side streets and up Avenida Prestes Maia. That's what I liked. I was on my way to football. Wearing the team shirt. Cool breeze on my face. Cutting the air and the traffic in half.

It didn't last long though. Soon we ran into traffic, slowed down, and stopped. We sat there for ages in the middle of the hot cars waiting to get across the avenue. There were still two or three kilometres to go. The bus was creeping along so slowly I began to wonder if we were going to make it to the park on time. Then something hit me. It was water, splashing off my head. I spun round. The woman with the pink hair was cycling past on this orange bike, squirting at me from a water bottle.

'Sorry!' she said. 'It was an accident!'

'Thanks!' I called back. 'Just what I wanted to cool me down!'

Deni was shrieking with laughter.

'You think you're Mr Clever up there, don't you?' said the woman. 'Well, don't ask me to push your wheelchair when you fall off!'

'You'll fall off that bike first!'

'I don't think so, kiddo!' she shouted back. Then she cut round the side and was gone up the road faster than the cars or the bus or anything. We made it across the junction at last. Deni was still grinning from ear to ear.

'You look more like a wet lettuce than a team captain!' he called out.

I was just interested in trying to see up the road ahead. It was clear. We'd probably make it. But, as we picked up speed, Deni got it into his head to start whooping like a cowboy who's drunk too much coffee. Somebody on the bus must have heard. Because next stop, the driver got out.

I knew him. We'd taken lifts on his bus before. He was a short, round guy with a big balding head. He looked like a pregnant goat coming towards us. The thing is, though, we weren't going to let him see us hanging off the back. As soon as his door opened we'd got down. By the time he reached us, we're standing at the edge of the road.

'Don't you halfwits even think about touching my bus!' he said, pointing a big, fat finger.

'I wouldn't if you paid me,' I said back. '*It's filthy*!'

'Yeah. *Keep your hair on*,' added Deni. We're just crossing the road to visit my grandma.'

'Yeah?' nodded the driver, looking over the road at a bunch of men unloading cement off a lorry. 'She works on that building site, does she?'

Deni nodded.

'She's knitting curtains for the flats when they're finished,' he told him.

The driver sniffed and pointed again.

'Touch my bus and I'll knit your ears together and kick you all the way home!'

Then he walked back and got on. And as soon as the bus pulled off, we jumped back on, too.

We swung out into the traffic heading along the river. That was normally the best bit – flying along up high above the water. But it didn't happen. Another bus was coming up behind us. And that was it. The other driver honked. He flashed his lights. Both buses pulled over, and we had no chance. One driver was coming one way. The other was coming the other. Deni stumbled as he jumped, and dropped his bag. I could have picked it up. But I didn't. I didn't have time. There was a break in the traffic. I ran.

Cars beeped as they flashed past, but I made it over to the crash barrier along the riverbank. Deni missed the chance. He got stuck on the other side of the road. When I looked back, one of the drivers had him by the neck of his T-shirt. The other grabbed his throat. They were shouting. Then he twisted suddenly. The T-shirt ripped. Deni was away! He was faster than the drivers. And there was too much traffic for them to get anywhere near *me*. One of them picked up Deni's football bag and kept it. Next thing, the buses were pulling away.

The sun beat down on my head. I looked about. There was no sign of Deni. And there was no chance of getting to training on time now. I kicked a stone in the river. You could smell the stink of the water. It was full of dumped junk and stuff coming out of the sewers. There was even a bike down in the mud.

'Why d'you go and do that?' came a voice. It was Deni.

'What?' I asked.

He rested his arms on his knees to catch his breath. 'You wriggled off like a snake, and left me on my own!'

The traffic sped past. I shrugged.

'You didn't even pick up my bag! That was my football kit! And look what they did to my shirt!'

'You should've run, too!' I told him. 'And you should've shut your big mouth on the bus. Now we're going to miss training.'

'Senhor Jonas isn't going to be happy with you, is he?'

'I'm the captain,' I said. 'That means I'm in the team whatever.' Then I looked down at the river. 'I'm going to get that bike.'

'You'll fall in and die,' Deni told me.

'I won't,' I said, and started scrambling down. 'I'm going to get it out and fix it.'

I had to reach right into all the scummy water to get hold of the bike. But I pulled it out and wheeled it back up to the road.

'Don't even touch that!' Deni shouted. 'It stinks!'

He was right. But it didn't look that old or broken. One tyre was still hard.

'It's a pile of junk!' tutted Deni, kicking the back wheel.

'Get off it!' I said, and shoved him in the chest. 'I'm going home.'

'So am I,' tutted Deni. 'But not with you. You smell like a donkey now!'

He went striding off. But I didn't mind. I was happy with the bike. I hadn't had one for ages.

Aunt Rosângela was out when I got home. She works in a hotel. Sometimes in the day and sometimes at night. I live with her because my dad went off a long time ago and I don't know what happened to my mum. My aunt won't tell me. She just says she's going to look after me because she was Mum's big sister. And whenever she says that, it sounds like I won't see Mum again.

I was hungry, so I went to the bakery. They always give me a cheese bread or something.

I don't even have to ask. Senhor Jonas lived above that bakery when he was a kid. He says he used to play football *in* our street. I don't know when that was, but it must have been ages ago because if you play there now you'll be hit by a car. You're lucky if anyone even lets you play out on the pavements, because of all the crack-heads and beggars. That's why Senhor Jonas set up football training. So kids from neighbourhoods round where he grew up can still play football, and maybe become professional like he did.

Nothing was going to stop me getting to training the next day. My aunt gave me the bus money. I didn't go round to Deni's or anything. I stood in the heat at the stop. The bus came. I got on the normal way. But I never expected it to be the same driver. The pregnant goat.

I tried to get past without him looking. But he said, 'D'you think I'm dumb as a stump?'

'What?' I asked. But he got up and stopped me with his sweaty arm.

'Get off!' I called out.

'You're the one getting off!' he told me.

'I've got my bus money to pay,' I said. 'I've got to get to football!'

He shook his head.

'And don't think you'll get on the next one, either. It's my mate from yesterday driving it.'

I had to get that bus or the next one or I wasn't going to get to training on time. But the driver was shoving me. I went back down the steps. Everyone stared.

'Go home and watch TV!' said the driver. *'The Muppet Show*'s on at five o'clock!'

Walking home, I thought what Senhor Jonas was going to say. When you missed *one* training he didn't like it. Now I hadn't shown up twice in a row. And if he found out it was because I'd got caught riding the back of the bus, he'd explode. It was hot indoors, so I went outside. I pulled off my football shirt and chucked it on the ground. I tried fixing the bike. I managed to wash most of the mud off. But I didn't know how to get the brakes to work. And I didn't have any way to pump up the tyre. I gave up. I couldn't do it. I pushed the bike over and I kicked it even harder than Deni did.

It was getting dark. But the air wasn't any cooler. I sat in the doorway and stared at the cars, the motorbikes, the taxis ... the men laughing in the bakery ... the crack-heads using the wall of the car park for a toilet ... people hurrying home. Then *there was Senhor Jonas*! He got out of his car. He looked at me and came across the road.

'Juca,' he nodded. I nodded back. 'Where've you been?'

'I couldn't make it,' I shrugged.

'You've got to train.'

'I know.'

'What happened?'

'I got a cold.'

'Yeah?'

Senhor Jonas looked away. Then he looked back and shook his head.

'It's true. I got ill. I couldn't make it. I'll be there tomorrow.'

'Tomorrow's Friday. The next training's Saturday.'

'I know,' I told him. 'I'll be there Saturday.'

'If your cold's better.'

I looked at the ground. Senhor Jonas bent down.

'You don't have to give me *stupid excuses*, Juca,' he said. 'You could be a very good footballer. And I thought if I made you captain, you might

113

get your act together. But if you don't train ... and you can't even look me in eye and tell me the truth, I'm not interested.'

'Interested in what?'

'In having you in the team.'

This time *I* shook my head.

'I'm the captain,' I told him. 'I'm in the team. You know I'm in the team.'

'I don't know,' said Senhor Jonas, and he picked my shirt off the floor. 'Everyone's got to earn one of these.'

'That's mine!' I said.

But he kept the shirt and walked off.

'You've got to earn it, Juca!'

Then he crossed the road and drove away.

I couldn't stop thinking about it. What could I do if the drivers wouldn't let me on? Hang off the back of the bus again? Run all the way to the park? The bike was the thing. I woke up in the morning knowing I had to fix it. My aunt sent me over to the bakery to get milk and I stood in the queue, working out how to do it. I knew where there was a cycle shop and I decided to take the bike down there. On the way, I met Deni. He was with his cousin Robson. He looked at the bike, and started laughing.

'You said you were going to fix that!'

'I am,' I told him. 'I need it. They wouldn't let me on the bus yesterday.'

'You missed training *again*?'

I nodded.

'Then Senhor Jonas came round. He said maybe I wasn't even in the team any more.'

'I told you!' shouted Deni. 'He's got a screw loose! Mind you. You *were* a crap captain.'

Robson started laughing. I pretended I was going to slap Deni on the head. But I didn't.

'Forget about football training,' said Deni. 'I'm not going. It's not as good any more.'

'I'm still going,' I told him.

'On that bike?' asked Deni.

I nodded.

'I'm taking it down to that bike shop.'

Robson shook his head. 'They won't fix that,' he shrugged. 'It's full of expensive bikes in there.'

'I'm going to ask them,' I said.

'They won't do it,' laughed Deni. 'Come with us. There's a party at the church.'

'We're going to charge people for keeping an eye on their cars,' nodded Robson.

I shook my head. Then, even though I didn't want them to, they came with me to the shop and stood outside joking about as I pushed the bike in.

It *was* full of expensive bikes. The man had two customers with him, but he looked across at me.

I said, 'I've got this bike that needs fixing.'

He shook his head. 'I'm not interested.'

'I need it.'

'Sorry. These are all top-of-the-range, imported bikes. I don't touch that sort of thing.'

There was sweat on my forehead. 'It needs fixing,' I said.

'I can see that!' he told me. 'But I don't repair bikes that are stolen, or anything like that. Take it somewhere else.'

I told him that I'd found it. He smiled and said he was busy and opened the door for me to go out.

The boys fell about laughing at me.

'Let's go down the church,' said Deni. 'It's easy. You just sit there and people pay you. You don't even have to watch their cars.'

I didn't know what I was going to do. But I wasn't going to the church with them. So I walked off in the opposite direction. When I got to the hairdressers, I leant the bike against the steps and went inside.

It was the same two women working. The blonde one was doing someone's nails. The one with pink hair was sweeping up.

'Your guardian angel hasn't given up on you yet, then?' she said.

'What?' I asked.

'You haven't fallen off a bus.'

I shook my head.

'What do you want?'

'I want to know something,' I told her.

'You want me to fix you up with a pink hairstyle,' she said with a smile.

'*No*,' I told her, and they all burst out laughing. 'I've got a bike. I want to know if anyone can make it work because I need it to get to football training.'

The woman nodded and said, 'I'm after something, too. I need someone to clean our window.'

I looked at it. My drawing was still there, though it was just like a brown smudge now.

'You going to do it?' asked the woman.

'Do you know someone who can fix my bike?' I asked.

'Clean the window and you'll find out.'

'I don't know how to clean windows,' I said.

She put down her broom, got me a bucket of water and a squeegee thing on a pole and showed me what to do. It was easy. I was in the middle of doing it when I heard Deni's voice. From what he was saying, the priest had paid them something to clear off and stop bothering people down at the church. And he and Robson were coming down the pavement drinking milkshakes.

'What the hell are you doing now, Juca?' he asked.

'Cleaning this window,' I said.

'What? One moment you're captain of the football team. Next moment you're working at the hairdressers!'

I didn't laugh. 'Just clear off. I've nearly finished,' I said.

But Deni was already giving his milkshake a squeeze so that it came squirting out. Some of the milk went on the pavement. Some of it went on the window. Then Robson started doing it, too. And I didn't even think. I swung the bucket round and emptied it over the two of them. Deni tried one more squirt, but he'd backed off too far for it to hit the window. Then both the hairdresser women came out, and the boys ran off laughing.

'I'm sorry,' I said, wiping at the mess they'd made.

'I know the feeling,' said the woman with pink hair. Then she squatted down to look at my bike. 'Where do you live?'

'Just opposite the bakery.'

I pointed. She nodded.

'I can fix this myself. Finish the window and I'll stop by on my way home.'

And she did. She cycled round after they closed the shop. I found out her name is Silmara. It didn't take her long. She had tools to attach the brake cables and took the wheel and tyre off to find punctures. Then she checked the gears and adjusted the saddle so it was right for me. Finally, she put oil on the chain. I tried the bike out. It was good.

'How do you know how to do all that?' I asked.

'I'm a cyclist. I know about bikes,' she shrugged. Then she said, 'If you want to try it out properly, I'll take you on an adventure.'

'What adventure?' I asked.

She gave me the same smile she'd given me in the shop.

'Follow me,' she said, 'you'll find out.'

Then she got on her bike. And I pedalled after.

There was the usual end-of-the-day traffic jammed up and down the road. We cut straight through. Silmara kept looking round to see if I was still behind and I was. We headed out of the city centre up Rua Consolação. It's steep, but not anything as bad as what Senhor Jonas gets us to do.

Then, when we got to the top, she swung round onto Avenida Paulista and I couldn't believe it. There were loads of people on bikes. Maybe two hundred all gathered at the end of the avenue. Silmara looked round,

'Welcome to the adventure!' she said. 'We meet here the last Friday of every month. In a bit we'll be cycling off around the city. It's a campaign to try and get more space for bikes in São Paulo.'

I loved it. There were flags and hooters and flashing lights on the bikes. Some people were in fancy dress. One had a weird double-decker bike that meant he was sitting right up high.

And, when we cycled off, everyone started shouting, 'MORE BIKES! LESS CARS! MORE BIKES! LESS CARS!'

And there I was. Cool breeze on my face. Gliding along in the middle of that crowd. Cutting the air and the traffic in half.

The next day I cycled over to football. And I was one of the first to arrive. Senhor Jonas was busy setting up the goals, but I know he noticed me as I went past. The others came to see my bike as I leant it against a tree.

'It's a top-of-the-range imported model,' I told them.

Senhor Jonas didn't say anything. He reached into his bag, got out my shirt and threw it so it hit me in the chest. I pulled it on and started to warm up.

What We Love
by Julia Green

We run up the four flights of steps, because the lifts aren't working, as usual. We race, and I'm first. My feet clatter along the concrete corridor.

Jasmeena's mum is already opening the door to the flat. 'What a racket!' She smiles at me. 'Hello, Suna! Come on in, you two. How was school?'

'Fine!' Jasmeena says, pushing me into her bedroom before I can start on a proper reply. She doesn't like me talking to her mum because I answer all the questions that she won't!

Jasmeena turns on the computer so we can chat with everyone on MSN. We watch some funny clips about cats, and then we go onto the balcony and watch everything that's happening, way down below. People look tiny from up here, and the cars are like toy ones, and you can imagine what it's like being a bird.

Most days after school I go back to Jasmeena's, or she comes to mine. We live on the same estate, but in different blocks of flats. Her flat is on the top floor: you can see for miles, right out over the River Thames. At night it's really brilliant – I love the way the lights make ribbons along the roads, and all the offices and houses are lit up, and the fairy lights along the bridges make reflections on the dark water. The flat is so high up, it's like living in the sky.

Jasmeena and me have been friends since we were about six. She is beautiful, with long dark hair and thin, graceful hands and feet that are always dancing. But she doesn't like school much. Me, I love it. I like making things and finding out new stuff and writing stories and we do lots of that with our teacher, Mr Brooks.

'So,' Jasmeena says, as we go back inside and flop down on her bed, on the pink quilt. 'What do you want to do?'

'Homework first,' I say, 'and then we can relax afterwards.'

Jasmeena's mum knocks on the door but she comes straight in anyway, without waiting for us to say she can. She's carrying a tray with two glasses of cranberry and pomegranate juice, two slices of toast, and two oranges, cut into segments. 'There you go, girls,' she says. She looks around the room quickly, as if she's checking we haven't been doing anything we shouldn't, and when she sees Jasmeena's school books on the bed she looks relieved. 'You must finish all your school work, girls, before you play together,' she says.

Jasmeena frowns. She's about to snap at her but luckily her mum's already on the way out, closing the door behind her.

'Your mum's only being nice,' I say, picking up a slice of buttery toast. 'You should be nicer back.'

'She always says the same thing,' Jasmeena says. 'And we don't *play*. She thinks we're still six years old.'

Our homework is to make a list of things we love about living in a city. And then the things we don't like: *pros and cons*, ready for a class debate.

'Friends, obviously,' I say.

Jasmeena writes it down.

'You have more friends in a city because

everyone lives closer together and there's more people. Like, I can walk to your flat, and Michaela's, and Marek and Jamal are just round the corner...'

'Point made,' Jasmeena says. She chews the end of the pen, and the ink makes her lips black. 'What else?'

'Shops. Loads of.'

We count them. Just in the one street that goes from our estate to the train station, there's about three different kinds of deli, a flower shop, a mini-market, a wine shop, second-hand shop, posh clothes shop, estate agent, bank, pharmacy, three takeaways and Joe's Café. Plus all the market stalls, on Saturdays.

'In the countryside,' I say, 'there would be maybe one shop, selling groceries and stamps. Or just a farm, or something.'

'What else?'

'Probably nothing,' I say. 'Not even a post office.'

'NO, what else can I put on the list?'

'Buses every fifteen minutes. Trains. The zoo. Millions of museums and art galleries. Boat rides on the river. Parks.'

Jasmeena wrinkles up her nose. She doesn't write down any of those things. I watch her hand, slowly forming the letters *m a r k e t*.

'Which one? The flower market or the antiques market or the fresh fruit and veg market or the new one with French stuff?' I ask her.

She adds an 's'. 'All of them.'

It's almost time for *Neighbours*, so we do the second list quickly and I do the writing down this time. *Traffic. Pollution. Terrorists...*

'What!' Jasmeena interrupts. 'Terrorists?'

'You don't get them in the countryside, do you?' I say very sensibly. 'There wouldn't be any point!'

'How many terrorists have you ever seen?'

'It's just theoretical,' I say. 'Anyway, you might live right next door to one and you wouldn't know, would you?'

We think of some more things for the list. *Queues. Rush hour. Rubbish. Dogs.*

'What do you mean, dogs?'

'You can't have a dog if you live in the city,' I say.

'Loads of people do,' Jasmeena says. 'There are millions of dogs. It's just *you* who isn't allowed a dog. Cos your dad says.'

127

I huff. My dad. Exactly. He says a dog needs a house with a garden, and fields and woods to run in, and someone at home all day to look after it, and that it would be cruel to keep a dog in a flat like ours, even a very small one. And I don't want a small dog, I want my dream dog, which is a black-and-white Border Collie with a waggy tail and ears that prick up when it listens, and intense intelligent eyes the colour of Jaffa cakes. Her name will be Molly.

I draw her, very small in the corner of the page, looking straight out at me.

'Knife crime and drugs,' Jasmeena says, in a last desperate rush of inspiration before we go and watch telly.

Her mum comes out of the kitchen just as she says those words. 'My goodness! Whatever are you two talking about?'

'Just homework,' I explain. 'And,' I say to Jasmeena, 'people get murdered in the countryside, too. It's all exaggerated by the newspapers, anyway.'

The minute I get home, I know something's wrong. Dad's standing in the kitchen, opening a bottle of wine. The table has been laid with knives and forks and spoons, and there is the smell of spicy chicken wafting from the oven.

'It's a Thursday,' I say, looking at Dad. 'What's going on?'

'We're having a bit of a celebration,' Dad says, grinning from ear to ear.

Mum comes in. She's wearing a dress, and lipstick! She's even put her hair up.

'Will someone tell me what's going on?' I demand. I don't know why, but a little knot has tied in my tummy, like when you're about to do a spelling test.

Mum puts her arms around Dad's waist. 'Your clever father,' she says, 'has got a new job!'

I look at him. That isn't all, is it? I know there's more.

'Which means we can move out of this flat, at last!'

'To where?' I say. I *like* this flat. I don't want to move anywhere. I've lived here all my life. That's *ten* years. Nearly eleven.

'The new job's based in Wales,' Mum says. 'Isn't that lovely? We'll be close to the hills and not far from the sea. I'm so excited!'

And hundreds of miles away from my friends, and my school, and all the things and people I love.

Mum's got her back to me, as she mashes sweet potato in a pan on the stove. Dad's pouring two glasses of wine. They don't see my face.

I can't believe they're doing this to me. I storm out of the kitchen and slam my bedroom door. I turn on the computer to send messages to Jasmeena, and then Michaela and Sam and Jamal. *I'll come round right now,* Jasmeena messages back. *No,* I reply. *Later. Got to have Family Dinner.* I click on the sad-face icon.

After a while, Mum comes in and sits on the end of my bed. 'It's a shock,' she says. 'I know all your friends are here. But you can stay in touch. Emails, texts, it's easy these days. Jasmeena will just be a train journey away. She can come down every holiday. You can visit her.'

She hasn't a clue, my mum.

My parents are so excited that it's hard to be as cross as I really am. My dad will earn more money. We can have a proper house with loads of rooms, instead of a flat. Mum's even thinking about doing bed and breakfast, cos it's the sort of place where people go for holidays, apparently.

'I'm just about ready for a change of job, after all those years at the office,' Mum says. 'I've always fancied running a little B&B.'

I feel so sick I can't eat any chicken dinner, even though it's my favourite.

Jasmeena turns up at the front door half an hour later. She comes in and flops next to me on the sofa. She puts her arms round me and we both cry, and it's not because of the silly programme we're only half watching. It's like my heart is breaking.

Over the next few weeks, I seem to see everything differently, now I know I'm leaving it behind. The way the sky looks in the evening, when the lights are just beginning to come on. The sounds of sirens: ambulance and police cars, woven with the steady hum of traffic, and aeroplanes; blasts of music as someone opens a car door or a window in one of the flats in our block. It's the soundtrack of city life, familiar and comforting because it's what I've grown up with since I was a baby. When I'm at school, my eyes keep going to the display we made after the class debate about

Pros and Cons of City Life. Our list of what we like is miles longer than the things we don't. It seems most of us are happy here.

When I think of living in the country, all I imagine is empty fields, and mud, and having to have lifts from Mum if I go anywhere, and some tiny school with children who are nothing like me. I'll be like the alien from outer space. I won't have any friends. Bit by bit, Jasmeena will drift away, and soon she'll forget all about me...

She swears she won't.

We sit in Joe's Café one Saturday. The windows are all steamed up and it's cosy and noisy as Joe fries bacon for breakfast butties and banters with the customers, who are mainly people from the market. We sip our chocolate mocha milkshakes with orange straws and I think there is nothing more delicious in the world.

'Cheer up, sugar. It might never happen!' Joe says when he sees my mopey face, and I say back, 'It already has.'

He laughs. He lets us have two doughnuts for free.

We dawdle through the market, looking at all the stuff on the stalls. Jasmeena's supposed to be buying fruit for her mum. I help her choose mangoes and melon and strawberries. We drift along to the jewellery stall, and try on rings and bracelets.

'Which one do you like the best?' Jasmeena asks me, and when I pick out the silver ring with a turquoise stone she hands it to the lady, with the money, and then passes the white paper package to me. 'For friendship,' she says. 'Wear it for ever.'

It starts to sink in. We really *are* leaving the city. It's actually going to happen. Dad and Mum pore over leaflets with house details. They go off for trips to Wales to look at houses. Finally, they show me a picture of the house they like the best. 'What do you think, Suna?'

I stare at the photo of a stone house, with a garden all the way round, and chimneys and a wooden fence and a gate and everything, like in a storybook. I shrug. 'It's OK.'

Mum sighs. I know she wants me to be excited like she is. 'Four bedrooms!' she says. 'A proper garden! A garage, and a shed. And it's on a bus route, and only twenty minutes' drive from the train station.'

Jasmeena and I look on Google Earth at the

new place: green, basically, with loads of trees, and a river, and a few houses dotted about. The knot in my tummy ties a bit tighter.

Jasmeena looks at me. 'It'll be OK,' she says. 'I'll come and visit, and you can come here and stay with me any time you want. Promise. Cross my heart and hope to die.'

I hug her. My eyes are all teary again.

'There's one good thing,' Jasmeena says.

'What?'

'You can have your dog. Look – there's a big garden. Fields for walking. Your mum at home in the day, doing her beds and breakfasts. Your dad can't possibly say no now.'

It's not a very fair swap, a best-friend-in-the-world and an exciting, bustling, colourful place you love and know so well you could get round it with your eyes shut, in exchange for a dog. But the day we go to pick up Molly, exactly one week after we move into the new house at the end of the May bank holiday, my broken heart starts to mend.

I text Jasmeena:

Choosing puppy 2day! CU l8r.

I email her as soon as we get back:

She is tiny and cute and furry, with black-and-white face and white tummy, and white paws with black spots. She is a Border collie cross. Her dad was probably a springer spaniel. She is eight weeks old and she chewed the newspaper all the way home and did a wee on the kitchen floor. She already comes when you call her. Her name is Molly.

I send a photo, too.

Jasmeena phones me right back. 'She's soooo sweet! Can I come down? Like, at the weekend?'

'YES!' I can hardly wait to see her again.

The first week I couldn't get to sleep at night because of all the noises. I thought it was going to be dead quiet, but it's SO not. A lady fox sits in our garden and screams as if she's being murdered. (First time, I thought it *was* someone being murdered. I was TERRIFIED!) Owls hoot like in a horror movie. The house creaks and groans and a million insects tick and scratch like they're eating away the walls. They probably are. From the minute it starts to get light (before 5 o'clock!) there are a trillion birds making the most awful racket. Black-and-white cows thunder along the edge of the field opposite and make the most horrible smells. They are more polluting than cars, even. That's a fact. We looked it up on the internet, me and Dad.

I warn Jasmeena about all the noise, when we're padding upstairs to my room. She could have her own, but we want to be together the whole time so we can talk. We've got so much to catch up on.

Molly pads behind us. She can't get up the stairs (she's too little, and she's not really allowed, either) so I pick her up and carry her and she licks my neck with her little pink tongue. It tickles.

'I'm going to train her properly,' I tell Jasmeena. 'So she walks to heel and comes when I whistle, and sits and stays and everything. She could be a working dog, so if she's a pet I have to make sure she's busy and has lots of exercise because they're really intelligent and when they get bored they get naughty.'

'Bit like Sam, at school.' Jasmeena laughs. 'Perhaps Mr Brooks should take him for walkies!'

She tells me about what they're doing at school for the last term. Everyone will be moving up to the Community College in September. For a moment I miss everyone so much I could cry, but I don't.

'I've visited my new school, too,' I tell Jasmeena. 'It's quite nice. There's a school bus that will pick me up from outside here. You can do canoeing and climbing and stuff like that on Friday afternoons.'

'Cool,' Jasmeena says.

'And I've got to learn Welsh.'

'Well,' Jasmeena says. 'That's a new one.'

In our old class, with Mr Brooks, we spoke 24 languages between us. When he calls the register, the class have to answer in a different language each week, which means we all know how to say *Good Morning* and *Yes* in Urdu, Portuguese, Polish, Arabic, Bengali, French, Pujabi, Yoruba, Swedish... But we haven't learned Welsh.

My mum's French Canadian and Dad's from Jamaica, originally, but I was born in London and now I live in Wales. So what does that make me?

Just me, I reckon: Suna.

I lie back on the pillows. Molly has curled herself up with her nose in one of my ballet pumps, fast asleep.

Jasmeena's sitting on the window seat, staring at the fields and the little birds flitting in and out of the tree, where there's a nest. She sighs. 'So much space!' she says. 'It's gorgeous, Suna. The house and the garden and the view and everything!'

It does all look better now she's here. I almost feel proud, later, when I show her the footpath down to the river, and the mass of pink-and-white wild flowers, and the place where you can jump across stepping stones to the other side, to the perfect place for a picnic. I show her the rope swing Dad tied to a high branch, and we take turns to swing out and back and round and it's so much fun we almost die laughing.

I guess you can get used to anything, really. And what we love, well that can change, too. Though some things won't ever change. I twist the silver and turquoise ring on my finger. Friendship, for example. That's for ever and ever, like Jasmeena said. Wherever you live.

About the Authors

Joanna Nadin
is a former broadcast journalist and Special Adviser to the Prime Minister. She has written several books for younger readers, including *Jake Jellicoe and the Dread Pirate Redbeard* – a Blue Peter book of the month and Lauren Child's pick of the year on Radio 4's Open Book – and *Maisie Morris and the Whopping Lies*, winner of the Lancashire Fantastic Book Award. She is also author of the acclaimed **Rachel Riley** series for teenagers. She lives in Bath with her daughter.

Ian Beck
began his career in the late 1960s as an illustrator. Among many commissions, he illustrated the cover for Elton John's album, *Goodbye Yellow Brick Road*. On the birth of his first child in 1981, he moved into illustrating children's books. He worked for many years illustrating collections of Nursery Rhymes and traditional folk and fairy tales.

Eventually, he began to write as well as illustrate, starting in 1989 with his picture book, *The Teddy Robber*. In the past six years he has moved away from picture books and written fiction for both middle years children and young adults. His first novel in the **Tom Trueheart** series, *The Secret History of Tom Trueheart Boy Adventurer*, has been translated into 19 languages so far and has been optioned as a live action film. His novel for young adults, *Pastworld*, was published in 2009 and has been optioned by Hollywood. Ian is a frequent visitor to schools and libraries throught the UK. He lives in west London.

T.M. Alexander

likes short words better than long ones and spinach more than cabbage. She writes in a study that no one knows exists, hidden behind a secret door pretending to be a bookcase. If the door ever gets stuck, she will never be seen again.

She is currently writing a series for children, called **Tribe**. The first two books, *Tribe: Jonno Joins* and *Tribe: Goodbye Copper Pie*, are on the shelves, and the third, *Tribe: Keener Bunks Off*, is coming soon.

Her short stories have been performed in Bristol (where she lives), London, and on BBC Radio 4.

She has been writing for five years, before which her smelliest job was frying donuts at a Sunday market.

When she's not writing, T.M. Alexander goes into schools and libraries with a big box of props to run story-making workshops. Find out more at www.tmalexander.com or www.tribers.co.uk

Born in 1953 in Warrington, Cheshire, **Alan Gibbons** has been writing full time for many years. He has won the Blue Peter Book Award and seven other book prizes. He has been shortlisted twice each for the Carnegie Medal (with *The Edge* and *Shadow of the Minotaur*) and the Booktrust Teenage Prize (with *The Edge*, *Caught in the Crossfire* and *The Dark Beneath*). Alan's latest book is *Scared to Death*, the first novel in the **Hell's Underground** series. Alan visits 150 schools a year and his books are published in nineteen languages. Alan lives in Liverpool with his wife and four children. You can find out more by visiting Alan's website www.alangibbons.com.

Sean Taylor
is the author of over 30 books for young readers, including the comic **Purple Class** adventures, which take place in an urban primary school, a collection of folktales from the Amazon called *The Great Snake*, and picture books for younger readers such as *Boing!*, *When a Monster Is Born* and *Crocodiles Are the Best Animals of All*.

As well as writing, he has many years experience visiting schools, where he works with poetry and storytelling to encourage young people to write themselves.

Sean grew up in Surrey, in the south of England, and at present lives in Brazil, where his wife is from and *Cutting the Air* is set. Find out more at www.seantaylorstories.com.

Julia Green's
novels for teenagers are *Blue Moon*, *Baby Blue*, *Hunter's Heart* (Puffin), *Breathing Underwater* and *Drawing with Light* (Bloomsbury). Her stories for younger children include *Over the Edge* (Pearson Longman), *Taking Flight*, *Sephy's Story* and *Beowulf the Brave* (A&C Black). Julia visits schools, libraries and festivals to talk about her

writing and to lead creative writing workshops for young people and adults. She has been a tutor for the Arvon Foundation. She is Senior Lecturer in Creative Writing at Bath Spa University and is the Course Director for the MA Writing for Young People. She lives on the edge of the city of Bath, close to the countryside, so she has the best of both worlds! You can find out more by visiting Julia's website www.julia-green.co.uk